D1411545

SECRET SEDUCTION

THE SECRET SERIES

JILL SANDERS

GRAYTON

To my extended family.
There are too many of you to list,
but you know who you are…
Thank you!

SUMMARY

To Katie life was simple. She wanted a little house in upper Boston, and four kids fathered by her best friend Jason, who she's been infatuated with since she was eight. After a devastating family secret is exposed, all she wants now is to escape the media hype that follows her everywhere she turns. Leaving her family, friends, and Jason behind, she travels to places she's only read about, to find a father she's never known.

Jason is on a mission and he's come halfway around the world to complete it. Despite his feelings for Katie, he won't let her resistance deter him, even if it means she'll never trust him again. As their world spirals out of control, their relationship will be tested and changed forever. If he can keep them alive and out of harm's way, he may have a chance to make everything right.

This is a work of fiction. Names, characters, places, and incidents either are the product of the author's imagination or are used fictitiously, and any resemblance to actual persons, living or dead, business establishments, events or locales is entirely coincidental.

SECRET SEDUCTION

DIGITAL ISBN: 978-1-942896-32-6

PRINT ISBN: 978-1-491272-32-9

Copyright © 2013 Jill Sanders

Copyeditor: Erica Ellis – inkdeepediting.com

PROLOGUE

atie Derby sat across from Jason and wondered why she had agreed to meet him at the coffee shop. She'd been embarrassed since Lynda's party several weeks ago when she'd gotten drunk and admitted to him all the years she'd had secret feelings for him. Then she had topped it off with a stupid kiss. One that he had held still through, very still. It had been apparent to her that he didn't feel the same way about her. Now she sat fidgeting with her napkin in her lap, wishing to be anywhere else on the planet.

"It's not that... Well, it's just that... I had never..." He was mumbling, and she could tell he was terrified. His beautiful blue eyes were searching her face.

"Jason," she interrupted him, trying to explain before he said something that would rip her heart out, "I don't want you to think – well, I was very drunk. It was just a mistake. I don't want there to be any weirdness between us." A little part of her heart broke off and floated to the floor when he looked almost relieved.

Before he could respond, her cell phone rang. Seeing her brother's number, she hit ignore. Not two seconds later, she saw her father's number and she hit ignore again.

Looking back at Jason, she noticed the fear in his eyes and could already tell the weirdness between them had settled in. She took a deep breath but wanted to pound her head on the table.

"Katie, I don't know..." Her phone rang for the third time. Looking down she saw her mother's number.

"I'm sorry, Jason, I better..." she nodded to her phone.

"Sure." He looked like he wanted to bolt for the door.

"Hello, Mom, what's so important?" she answered, stepping away from the table and walking towards the back of the almost empty coffee shop.

"Katie, oh thank God you answered. I wanted to talk to you before you heard a bunch of lies from anyone else."

Her mother cleared her throat and then continued on. "Well, sweetie, first of all, I wanted to tell you something, because I know it's going to come out very soon, and I thought you would want to hear the truth instead of the lies that are going around on the news or hearing something completely false from the police."

Katie waited, knowing that she wouldn't be able to interrupt her mother once she had started.

"Twenty-six years ago, after your father and I had a huge falling out, I went to Italy to recover from the pain your father had caused, and ... well... I had an affair with a man named Damiano Cardone. We had a son. I left them in Italy to come back and divorce your father, but he... well, we didn't get a divorce. Anyway, I kept in touch with them, and in a roundabout way, Damiano and I are married. Well, that's not the important part. Four years later I visited them and when I returned back home, I realized I was pregnant again and … well… this time I had you. Obviously, it was too late to keep it from your father, since he had already found out I was pregnant. He was just so happy about it."

Katie felt herself starting to hyperventilate.

"I just couldn't break your father's heart, so I made him believe you were his. Damiano Cardone is your biological father, honey, not Rodrick. I'm sorry I had to tell you over the…" Katie dropped her phone. Her ears were ringing, and her vision grayed around the edges. Jason was beside her, yelling at her to breathe. The last thing she saw before she passed out were Jason's blue eyes, hovering over her.

CHAPTER 1

*K*atie sat in the soft sand on the beach and thought about her life as the sun was setting. A strong and independent woman, she thought she knew what she wanted out of life. But then last year her mother had thrown a wrench into her carefully laid out plans. It had been a year since she'd seen or talked to anyone from her past life. The only thing that she still wanted, and had always wanted, was Jason.

Jason Keaton had been her best friend, and for one wonderful year, her roommate. He was the only man Katie had ever wanted to be with.

Now as she watched the sun setting over the water, she knew she had been naive. She had spent years of her life trusting people, only to find out that they had all been using her. Her friends had quickly turned on her, her mother had lied to her, Jason had even... well, that was more complicated. She didn't want to think about Jason. She'd tried and tried not to think about him for the last year.

Now she was sitting on a beautiful beach in a foreign country watching the bright colors of the sunset, and all she had to her name was the small backpack of clothes on her back. No apartment, no furniture, no friends, no one to tie her down.

She'd been to more places than she could count since leaving the states, from Paris to Madrid, and Berlin to Athens. She had spent the last year crisscrossing Europe and enjoying every minute of her venture.

The next day she had plans to meet her biological father, Damiano Cardone, for the first time. She didn't know who to trust anymore, so she had kept to herself since her mother's big reveal.

She didn't know if she would keep her meeting with her real father, or as she liked to call him, her biological daddy, or BD for short. The meeting was scheduled for the next day in his Athens office building. He owned one of Europe's largest businesses, New Edges. There were even branches of the business in the US run by his son, her biological brother Dante. Katie didn't quite know what the company did. Export, she thought, but she knew he was as powerful as the man who'd raised her was.

Rodrick Derby, the man she still thought of as her real dad (RD for short) had been just as deceived as she had. Believing his wife had been faithful to him for almost thirty years, he had raised Katie, not knowing the secrets his wife had been keeping.

Turning her thoughts to the other man who'd been lied to for years, she thought of what she could possibly say to Damiano. What could he say to her? They had both been robbed. Robbed of time and knowledge of each other's existence by a woman she no longer wanted to call her own flesh and blood.

Just then she heard a noise and quickly looked over her shoulder. The beach had grown darker and she couldn't see anything or anyone around her. The quiet beach was deserted. She could hear the surf hit the soft sand and enjoyed the mellow rhythm. She sat near the edge of the tall grass and looked to where the noise had come from, behind her, near the tree line. She realized this part of the beach was too far off the pathway for it to be another tourist. It might have been a local, or a deer or some other kind of animal.

She realized she was sitting alone in the dark, so she quickly stood up, dusted the sand from her jeans, and picked up her backpack. She started to walk back towards civilization and a row of hotels that she knew were just inside town. The tall buildings were lined up along the horseshoe-shaped beach and were no doubt full of tourists. Instead of stopping and getting a room when she'd gotten into town, she'd walked by them, straight to the beach, which had called to her. She'd walked right by all the happy families and couples enjoying the warm water and hot sun on the beach until she'd felt satisfied she'd worked out a few things in her mind. She'd ended up on the deserted part of the beach, alone.

She was desperately trying to find some answers to who she was, what she now wanted out of life. It had taken just over a year for her to contact Damiano. He was her biological father, and she was curious to meet the man.

When she had contacted him, Katie had been insistent that she didn't want her mother, Kathleen, there when she met him, so they had arranged a meeting at his Athens office. Damiano's voice had been strong, deep, and rich, and even with his accent, his words were easily discernible. He sounded eager for the meeting and she could tell he was just as nervous as she was.

She'd traveled to Athens via train and bus in under a week. But when she'd arrived, she had continued southwest until she'd hit the coastal town of Alimos. It was just a quick twenty-minute drive to Athens and Damiano's office, but she felt a little more level-headed staying outside the larger city, in a smaller, more secluded area.

Walking out of the tall grass area, she hit the soft, smooth sand and heard a twig snap right behind her. When she turned around to look, there was nobody around. Turning and picking up her pace a little more, she tried to keep her mind occupied by remembering the multiple day train ride south she'd taken. It had been a very nervous trip for her.

When she had left Denmark, her heart was light, her pulse pounding with adrenaline and excitement. She couldn't wipe the eager look off her face. A few days later, by the time she'd reached Greece, her feelings of excitement had been replaced with nervous dread. Her palms were sweaty, her face flushed, and she couldn't sit still in her seat. The beautiful scenery that passed her by in the train's large windows just didn't hold her interest anymore. She would sit and stare out at it, unseeing. Instead, visions of the meeting to come flashed before her eyes. What would he look like? Did she look like him? Would he be kind? How would she greet him? Should she give him a hug? Would he cry?

Several times, she had felt like everyone on the train had been watching her. After all, her face had been on every news channel last year in America. She'd had a hard time going anywhere without people pointing at her. When she'd gone to classes, the kids would make fun of her. Even at the grocery store, people in line would see her face on the tabloids and then look at her. Sometimes she would see a mix of pity and amusement in their faces. It wasn't as if she'd asked for all the attention, unlike some of the other women she'd seen on those same tabloids. She'd been thrust into overnight stardom thanks to her mother's infidelity and her family name.

Being the daughter of Rodrick Derby, the second of the prominent New England Derby's, was big news on its own. But when it turned out that she was actually the daughter of Damiano Cardone, entrepreneur of New Edges, a multimillion dollar company, she became even bigger news.

On the train trip there, she'd thought about getting off and heading someplace else. But she had never chickened out before in life and wasn't about to start now, so she had continued on her path. She didn't consider leaving the US as running away; instead, she chose to think of it as a necessary break.

She looked back down the beach to where she'd just come from, trying to see if someone or something was following her. She couldn't see anything except the water reflecting off the dark sky. Since it was a new moon, the clear sky was filled just with stars which, although bright, were not bright enough to light up the dark beach. It was too dark to see if there was anyone around. She felt the cool breeze hit her face and smelled the salt water and sand in the air. Although it was warm, she felt a shiver travel up her spine. She pulled her jacket closed and tried to keep her eyes and mind focused on the bright lights ahead of her.

Maybe there was a journalist following her? After all, the media had been almost unbearable back in the States; she'd been followed, photographed, and questioned every time she'd left her small dorm room back in Boston. They had exploited every detail of her life, including her friends, her party habits, and even the classes she was taking. They especially focused on the fact that she'd been going to school there for five years with no real end in sight. She had felt like her whole life was under a microscope.

The betrayal of her close friends had been immediate. For weeks after, they could be seen on every news station telling her life story and every detail of their friendship to anyone who would pay them enough. Even Brenda, her very best friend since second grade, had been seen on TMZ, exposing Katie's party habits. She had even told them that Katie didn't know what she wanted to do with her life. But it had taken seeing Jason's face on the television to make her pack a small bag and buy a one-way ticket to Europe.

That night, she had watched as he exited his car outside his dorm room, his dark sandy hair looking like he'd just run his hands through it. He hadn't shaved that morning, which always gave him a rough, boyish look Katie loved. He had been walking to the door when a swarm of reporters started yelling questions at him.

"How long have you and Katie Derby been seeing each other?" one shouted.

"When are you and Katie getting married?" another one could be heard.

"What is your relationship with Katie Derby?"

SECRET SEDUCTION

She could tell that the questions had taken him by surprise. Instead of keeping his head down, he looked into the camera. It seemed to take forever for him to start answering. Katie had gotten so upset when she heard his reply.

He had looked so dumb-founded, his blue eyes searching the crowd like he didn't know what was happening.

"Katie and I are just fr…"

He stuttered, almost as if it had taken all his conscious thought to try and figure out their relationship. She knew what they were, she could easily shout it from every rooftop. How hard could it be to say it to a bunch of strangers? They were best friends.

She'd been hurt, so hurt, that when she had slammed off the television, interrupting his statement, she had pushed the button so hard that it had caused the small set to fall off the stand. The set had wobbled at first and she thought about trying to catch it, but then she watched as it fell forward and landed hard, shattering the display in a million pieces. Glass and plastic had fallen all over her black-and-white polka dot rug, and she realized she didn't care.

Several girls stopped in the hallway and looked at her, then continued on their way, giggling, and no doubt talking about her.

That was the last time she had seen anyone she knew -- her friends, her family. She hadn't even officially dropped out of school.

She packed her small backpack, leaving everything behind: her new iPhone, her laptop, her designer clothes and shoes, everything. She took a cab to the airport and booked the next flight out, which just happened to be to Paris.

She had spent the last year of her life traveling around Europe, spending her savings, not once touching the credit cards from her old life.

She'd seen places she had always wanted to visit. Even though she kept to the smaller towns, the cheaper hotels, and the inexpensive restaurants, she had still been enjoying herself. And the main thing was, she'd kept her mind off her problems, at least when she'd kept busy.

Every time she had had some downtime over the last year, she had always reverted back to thinking about the betrayal, about her mother, her friends, and most importantly, Jason. She tried not to think about her problems too often. She wasn't really wallowing in pity, more like taking a break from reality.

Looking around her, she felt a little relieved that she'd hit the main pathway back into town. Here the wood planks of the walkway creaked under her feet. She could barely see the path leading to the lights and safety of the small city and couldn't even see her own feet in front of her, causing her to stumble a few times on uneven planks jutting out from the path. She thought she heard a board creak behind her and turned quickly to look. Seeing nothing, she quickened her pace. Was someone following her? She felt like she was being toyed with. In all her time being alone in Europe, she'd never felt threatened or scared. Now, however, she would have done anything to have a friend with her.

She could feel her fear vibrating throughout her entire body. Her hands shook as she held onto her backpack, and her breath was coming in quick bursts. She felt like running but didn't want to seem like one of those crazy women who went running and screaming because of a small noise.

When she reached the clearing of the first street and could finally see her own feet in the light, she started to relax and released a large sigh of relief. She had no time to scream as a black bag was tossed over her head, and she was grabbed by several large hands.

*a*s Katie watched the sun sink lower over the waters at Alimos, Jason watched her from the shadows of a small cluster of trees a few yards away. It was a quiet, peaceful night and the warm day had finally cooled off, leaving a slight chill in the air. He had been curious when she'd walked right through the town and straight to the beach. When getting into a new town, she normally would get a hotel room before she went exploring. This time, she had walked to the beach almost like she had a purpose. He had wondered if she'd spotted him several times during the short bus trip there.

He'd been only a few seats back. Since leaving Denmark, she'd been too preoccupied to even look around her. If she had, she would have easily spotted him on the trains and buses.

He remembered last year when he'd arrived back at her dorm room. Her place had looked like someone had broken in and gone through it. Katie was a huge neat freak and he knew instantly that something was wrong.

Her television was laying on the floor in pieces, her closet was ransacked, with some clothes missing and others tossed about the room. Half of her drawers were opened and empty.

They had been roommates two years ago and he had never heard the end of her complaints about his stuff lying around. Finally, she had just given up on him and started picking everything up herself. She had eventually moved back into the dorms because of his messy lifestyle. But shortly after she had left, he had become somewhat of a neat freak himself. He supposed it had taken her not being around to realize how sloppy he was, so he changed.

When he had walked into her dorm room that first day, he had been sure that something bad had happened to her. Then the girl that lived down the hall had walked by. The busty blond had been trying very hard in the last two years to get his attention. He'd never given her any, which had only made her work harder.

"It's too bad Katie left. We'll sure miss her around here." She leaned against the open doorway, and when she smiled at him, Jason almost felt his skin crawl.

"Left? What do you mean left?"

"Oh, yeah. She was watching you on TV and then went a little crazy and did that." She pointed to the shattered set and continued, "Looks like she didn't like seeing you get some of her spotlights. She packed her bags and left less than ten minutes later."

When the girl finally left, he stormed out of Katie's room and headed to her parents' house just outside of Boston. No one was there, and their live-in maid told him that she didn't know where Katie was, or where she was going.

It had taken him less than a day to call both of her parents and her brother. When a month had gone by and no one from her family had heard from her, he started to panic. He remembered hearing her tell him once that she wanted to travel to England, but he didn't know if she would actually do something like that.

Before he could make a decision about what to do, he received a call with some important information on her whereabouts, which had helped him make up his mind. So, he had purchased a ticket and set off to chase her across Europe.

When he had finally tracked her down, he had been only three days behind her. He had been so close, but then, she had dropped off the face of the earth again.

How could someone who had failed geography in high school -- twice -- move around a foreign country like she was born there?

He had known her forever and not once had she said anything about being interested in traveling like this. When she had talked about traveling, she had mentioned five-star hotels, the best restaurants, and expensive shops.

But instead, he had been following her through small towns, country roads, and small hotels. He had noticed she was keeping away from the larger cities and staying away from too many people, most likely trying to avoid the spotlight he knew she had hated in the states.

It had been just under a year since he'd followed her across the big pond, as the locals liked to call it. He'd spent nights in hotels, dives, and bed and breakfasts. Sometimes he had ended up sleeping in the small tent he had purchased.

But now he had finally followed her to Greece, where

17

he knew her biological father, Damiano, was visiting one of his many business offices. He followed her south to Athens, always keeping out of sight on the train. If she'd known he was there – well, he didn't want to think of what she would have done. She might have run; she might have been mad. He didn't know, but he knew he couldn't chance it yet.

Once, in a small cafe just outside of Barcelona, she had almost seen him. It had been the first time he'd been that close to her in almost a year. She'd looked good, very good. She'd cut her dark curly hair shorter and had short spiky bangs that accented her face and highlighted the fact that she'd lost a few pounds since the last time he'd laid eyes on her.

He had watched her walk across the street and purchase a few items in the small boutique. He swore to himself he'd never get that close again. It was too hard on him, seeing her, hearing her, smelling her. So he'd kept his distance from then on, following her farther back.

Until the night before she was supposed to meet her father. He'd been watching her from the darkness of the trees that sat a few yards away, as she sat on the beach. She looked so lonely, he had thought for a few seconds about going over there to comfort her. He'd thought about doing that a lot over the last few months. He knew her, she needed her space to work things out on her own. It was just killing him not to spend time with his best friend. He missed talking to her, missed being with her, missed her laugh.

Then he had heard something. He listened as two men approached slowly, whispering as they watched her, and he knew he had to come up with a plan quickly. So, he'd done what he'd been training his whole life for, and acted as quickly as possible to save her.

The bag smelled of rotten potatoes. The hands were rough and grabbed her in places she'd never let anyone touch her before. Screaming had been met with a mouth full of dust and cobwebs, so she'd quickly shut her mouth. She decided instead to try kicking out blindly, which she hoped would give her a chance of fighting them off. She was satisfied when she heard a loud grunt as her foot connected with something solid.

She was thrown down on the rocky ground and when she landed on her backpack, her head snapped back and hit a rock. She could taste blood in her mouth. Someone was sitting on her chest and she found it hard to breathe. Her hands were yanked above her head while someone tried to tie her feet with something, possibly a rope. She kicked out with renewed energy, making sure to never put her legs too close together so they couldn't get a rope around them. The man above her had slipped something cold over her hands. Were those handcuffs? When she heard the small click of them sliding into place, she knew she was in trouble.

The cold metal dug into her wrists and she was finding it harder to breathe through the dusty bag. She kept her eyes closed because grit was getting into them, causing them to tear up. She was panicked, and she could feel her heart beat so hard that she could hear it in her ears.

Suddenly the man's weight was lifted, and her hands were freed from above her head. She could hear grunting and shouting but didn't stop to figure out what was happening. Removing the bag with her cuffed hands, she threw it on the ground. Sitting on the cool ground, she could see three figures fighting. One man stood in the middle and was kicking out at two larger men. She got up and started to run towards the lights, screaming at the top of her lungs.

She made it several feet when arms came around her from behind, grabbing hold of her shoulders and spinning her around. She didn't have to think, she spun around and struck out. Catching the man off guard, she watched as he stepped back a full step, holding his chin in his hands. Then he stared at her with the lightest blue eyes she'd ever seen.

"Damn it, Katie," he rubbed his jaw and stared at her.

"J – Jason?"

He recovered quickly and grabbed her hands, then started pulling her towards a darkened side street.

"We need to get away from those two men. Damn it, Katie, pick up your feet and run."

Several people had come out of their small houses on the outskirts of town to see what was going on. Katie just stared at them as he pulled her down a dark alley.

"I am!" At least she was trying to. It must have been the lack of oxygen that was causing her head to swim. She felt like she couldn't really focus on anything. It seemed to her that they had been running for miles through the streets and she started having a hard time keeping up. They had passed all the houses and entered the main part of the city. Here the buildings were taller and closer together, and the street lights lit up the darkness. She looked at Jason's back as he pulled her down the street after street. His hair was longer, and it looked like he'd gained a little muscle since the last time she'd seen him. He had always been skinny, but now he looked like he was built.

Finally, after they had gone over a dozen more blocks, she pulled her hands free of his hold. They were standing a few feet away from the corner of two streets in a busier section of town. Cars zipped by and she noticed people walking all around them. The nightlife of Alimos was busier here.

"Jason, stop! W-what are you doing in Greece?" She looked down and realized she still wore the shiny pair of handcuffs.

"It appears as though I'm saving your ass, again," he said, smiling down at her.

A memory flashed in her mind. It had all started the summer when she turned eight and had gone to the country club swimming pool with her mother and brother, Ric, something they did almost daily during the hot summer days in Boston. This particular day, she'd been stuck swimming in the kiddie pool because her mother was too preoccupied to watch her in the larger pool.

If her mother would just let her take swimming lessons like her brother had, she could enjoy the large green slide that twisted in loops and sat on the large side of the deep pool.

The slide was something Katie had always wanted to try out. Ric was constantly going down it or jumping off the diving board. That day it had been easy to escape her mother's attention. She was flirting with the lifeguard and wasn't keeping a close eye on Katie.

She remembered focusing on the large slide as she walked over to it. She can't remember making it up the stairs or what she had thought about while sitting at the top. But she did remember the thrill of falling and spinning as she jetted down the slick surface towards the cool, clear water.

Jason hadn't been much older or bigger than her, but he had been an avid swimmer already. His light blue eyes had been the first thing she had seen as she lay on the side of the pool.

Her mother and the lifeguard had also hovered over her, but she paid them no attention and just looked at the boy who had saved her. His worried eyes focused on her and when he noticed she was okay, he smiled the nicest smile Katie had ever seen. His sandy dark hair was slicked back away from his tan face, and he had the cutest dimple right above his mouth on the right side.

Jason's mother had rushed through the growing crowd at that point and a dramatic scene had ensued. Everyone pawed and oohed over Katie, but her mind was totally focused on Jason, much like it had been focused on the slide just a few minutes earlier.

Finally, everyone had settled down, and Katie was forced to sit in the shade the rest of the day while her brother played in the cool water and her mother went back to socializing. Jason had sat next to her for a while, and she had fallen in love right there, under a large oak tree by the kiddie pool at the country club.

For the remainder of the summer, Katie trailed Jason around at the pool. She spent every moment of her time at the club hunting him down and following him, until finally, instead of trying to ditch her like he'd been doing, one day he started looking for her instead. He taught her to swim and she enjoyed the game of sneaking away from her mother to be with him.

After that summer, Katie didn't go anywhere without Jason; they were inseparable. It was the same all throughout school as slowly they became best friends. If anyone dared hint that they were anything but friends, they would set them straight quickly. And for years and years, Katie had kept her infatuation to herself.

"Not that again." She blinked her mind clear and frantically started to pull at her wrists, trying to get the tight cuffs off. "I've told you a million times, I was swimming just fine. If you hadn't jumped on top of me, I would have made it to the side of the pool all by myself." It was an old argument that no one ever won.

He grabbed her wrists and quickly unlocked the handcuffs, then dropped them and the key on the ground. Katie wiped her face and eyes clear, but she felt like she was covered with dirt and was beginning to feel as if she was in shock. Her mind was foggy, almost like she'd spent the whole day running. Her breath was still shaky, and she tried to level it by taking deep breathes.

"Where did you get the key?" She walked over to retrieve the keys and cuffs, looking at them with wonder. She was trying to keep her mind off the fact that she'd almost been kidnapped.

"Leave them, Kat." He reached for her hand again. "We better keep moving."

"No, I'm not going anywhere until I get some answers." She pulled her hand out of his warm fingers as she started to shake. "Why are you in Greece? Have you been following me? How did you get this?" She held up the key and looked at it.

She watched him look around and then he shook his head in frustration. She finally got a good look at him. His face was scruffy with a few day's growth, giving him a more dangerous, mysterious look, something she had never thought about him before. He was almost unrecognizable.

His faded jeans hung low on his hips and his dark jacket had sand all over it. He had a dark pair of running shoes on and she noticed the dark straps of a backpack hanging on his broad shoulders.

She hadn't seen him in a year and looking at him now was like seeing heaven. She'd missed him but looking at him also stirred questions deep inside her. She wondered how their relationship would be now. Would it be changed? Had she changed too much? Had he changed too much for her to recognize?

When he ran his hands through his hair in frustration, she saw her old Jason and was very glad.

She was relieved that he had come along when he had. She'd been in trouble, a lot more than just getting in too deep at the swimming pool. She dumped the handcuffs and key and waited until he focused on her face again, thinking about what could have happened if he hadn't come along.

How much more could he take? He'd been punched in the gut and his fists hurt from knocking one of the guy's teeth loose. Then Katie had given his jaw a good whack, and she might just have given him a loose molar for all his trouble.

Looking at her standing in the dark alley, he was actually proud that she'd knocked his jaw loose. She must have paid a little attention to some of the self-defense classes he'd forced her to take in junior high. Now he could see her starting to shake and her face looked paler than normal. What they needed now was a place to stop and think, so he could regroup. Looking around, he saw a cafe a few blocks away and tried to pull her in that direction.

"I grabbed the keys from the guy I left spitting out his teeth back there," he said, nodding in the direction they had come. "I've been trailing you since Bristol, and it appears it was a good thing, too."

She stopped dead in her tracks. "Bristol?" He could see her mind working, calculating.

She'd been in Bristol for the New Year's celebration. He'd lucked out when he had caught up with her there. It had only taken him five months to track her down after she had left her dorm room

She'd attended the masquerade ball at Flamingos. His heart had stopped when he'd seen the silver dress she'd been wearing. That's when he'd noticed she'd cut her hair shorter. He'd easily gotten close to her with his mask on and she hadn't even noticed he was standing next to her. He had kept silent, hoping that she wouldn't notice it was him, but ended up the evening just following her back to her hotel room. It had been so good to see her again. He'd gone to sleep that night dreaming of her.

Upon her empty stare now, he grabbed her hands again and started to pull her towards the cafe and the lights.

"Come on." He checked over his shoulder as they walked, and when they passed under a bright street light, he noticed that her hair was a mess of wild tangles and she had dirt on her face. Stopping at the corner, he pulled her close and tried to fix her hair with his fingers. She swatted his hands away and took off her backpack and handed it to him. Pulling out a brush, she tried to straighten the tangled mess herself.

He had always admired her dark hair, it seemed to always be shiny in any kind of light. Now he could see a hint of red streaks he knew she'd gained from all her time outdoors. Her skin was glowing with the extra sun she'd taken in, as well. But it had been especially wonderful to hear her voice again; he had missed hearing it for so long. Over the last few months, he'd been so focused on watching her that he had almost forgotten what she sounded like.

"Why are you trailing me, as you put it?"

"I'll tell you everything if we can just get inside." He pointed to the cafe.

There were over a dozen people crammed in the small place and he knew that they could easily hide in a back, dark corner somewhere.

"Fine, but then you're going to give me answers to all the questions I have." She pushed her brush back in her bag and took the bag from him. Then she stormed across the street and walked through the doors, leaving him smiling behind her. That was his old Katie-Kat, doing everything her own way, on her own terms.

atie watched Jason scratch his face as they sat in the crowded cafe. He looked at her over his cup of tea and she could see the worry in his eyes.

"When was the last time you shaved?" she asked, trying to break the mood. Leaning forward, she sniffed in his direction. "When was the last time you bathed?" She waved her hand in front of her nose, making fun of him.

He laughed and sipped his tea. "Are these some of the important questions you want me to answer?" She'd always loved that smile. It was quick and heart-stopping. His white teeth flashed, and so did the little dimple on the right side of his mouth.

She smirked at him and nibbled on the scone she'd ordered. The food and tea were doing wonders to help calm her nerves. The place was crowded and loud with chatter. They had found an empty booth near the back hallway and she started to really think about what had happened. Had those two men meant to rape her? She shivered at the thought. She'd been so naive, wandering a foreign country all by herself for the last year; she'd felt safe until tonight.

"You didn't stop in one place long enough for me to enjoy the scenery, let alone grab a hot shower," he joked, but she could tell that he instantly wished he hadn't said anything. The laughter in his eyes stopped, and she watched as his face reflected the dark thoughts she now had.

"Katie..." He reached for her hand, but she pulled it away and started to play with the strap of her bag. She knew what was coming next; she had prepared herself for it since setting the meeting with her biological father. The family wanted her back, and no doubt, someone had called him to bring her back. Her family knew her one weakness was Jason. The question now was, who had exploited it, and him?

"Jason, I know why you're here. You might as well tell me who it is."

"What are you talking about?" He tried to give her an innocent look. She wasn't buying it.

"Don't play stupid with me, just go ahead and rat out whoever it is. I'll find out sooner or later. Is it Ric?" She leaned forward. "My dad?" She laughed quickly. "My other dad?"

He looked at her and she knew he could see the hurt masked in her eyes.

"Katie..." He started to explain, but just then there were two loud pops and the front glass of the cafe shattered. Glass shards scattered everywhere, raining down over people. The loud noise had caused everyone in the cafe to hit the floor or start running towards the doors. There was a lot of screaming and running, and Jason grabbed her arm and started pulling her towards the back door.

"Wait, my bag!" she screamed as he rushed them down the narrow hallway and out the back door.

"Leave it!" he yelled over his shoulder holding onto her tightly. She tried to pull him to a stop, but he was almost a foot taller and more than fifty pounds heavier than her. She had no choice but to be dragged down the dark alley.

They ran down a couple more side streets, and Katie was totally turned around now. It was dark and the streets all started looking alike. For all, she knew they could be just around the corner from the cafe. But she trusted him; he had a great sense of direction, always had.

As they ran down the dark streets, she remembered that he'd always been the one to drive anywhere they had gone back in Boston. She'd lived in the city her whole life and still didn't know how to get downtown. The one time she had driven, they'd ended up in Brighton instead of downtown Boston. She'd argued they were only thirty minutes late that night for the party they'd been going to. It wasn't as if she'd ended up driving to New York or anything. But for months she hadn't heard the end of jokes about the whole ordeal. She kept trying to blame him since he was supposed to be her navigator, but he wasn't buying it. He'd given her directions and she'd just kept driving on the freeway instead of following what he was saying. He'd just laughed and had sat back to enjoy the drive.

Her mind snapped back now, and she looked at him. He kept looking over his shoulder like they were still being chased, but every time she looked back all she could see was darkness.

"Who--" she started to ask, only to be hushed by him as he pulled them into an opened door. He quickly closed it and she heard a small click. "Are we--"

"Shh." He placed his hand over her mouth and pulled her back against the wall. She felt cold bricks at her back and his warm, hard body against the front, pressed tightly up against her. They were both breathing hard and with his larger hand over her face, she was slowly hyperventilating and felt a wave of dizziness come over her. Reaching up, she pulled his hand away from her mouth and glared at him in the dark.

It was all becoming too much for her. She'd had an exhausting day and now they were hiding out in someone else's... looking around she realized they were in a small storage closet.

With her mouth and nose free, she could smell his musky scent that she'd always enjoyed. He was still pinning her to the brick wall with his other hand, and she instantly felt that familiar flutter that always overtook her when she was around him.

She remembered the first time she'd ever felt that way about him. They'd gone to a party in junior high and had played Twister. She'd been winning, and it was down to just three people left: Katie, Jason, and Maggie Travis. Two moves later Maggie lost her footing on the blue circle. Since Katie had taken gymnastics, the game had been very easy for her. She could easily bend and twist her small body around to fit on any colored circle.

But then Jason had made a move that had put his chest right in her face, and she had made the mistake of inhaling his scent. He'd worn cologne that night, something she knew he had done on purpose because he'd wanted to impress Maggie. Instead, it had turned *her* knees weak and she'd ended up losing the game, with him hovering over her, smiling down at her.

Ever since that night, every time she got a good whiff of him, her knees turned to Jell-O. She thought how unfair it was that he had that power over her.

Looking up at him, she noticed that his blue eyes were focused on the doorway. He held very still and was breathing slowly. Looking over his shoulder, all she could see was a dim street light coming from under the locked door. She couldn't hear anything, and she was glad he was holding her up against the wall, keeping her from sliding down the cold stones to the colder floor.

There were a million questions running through her mind. First and foremost, had those been gunshots? Were the shooters the same guys that had just tried to kidnap her? Why her? What were they after? She didn't have any money on her. She remembered leaving her pack. If they wanted anything from her, they had just gotten everything she owned, except her backup credit card.

Wanting to bang her head against the wall, she looked at Jason again. He must have thought that whoever shot at the cafe was after them. Otherwise, he wouldn't be acting like they were being chased. Maybe he knew something she didn't? Is that why he was here?

More questions ran through her mind. Finally, after what felt like forever, she could feel Jason start to relax. His breathing changed, his stance changed, and even his hand on her shoulder dropped away. She instantly missed its warmth.

She held still, realizing she had gripped his jacket and she was holding him to her. She thought about letting go, but instead just held on to him, looking up into his face. He was beautiful. She'd always loved his smile; it was the second thing she'd noticed about him, after all. Now she looked at his mouth and wished she knew what it would feel like on her skin, on her lips, and she felt a shiver run down her spine. Could she make him want her like she wanted him?

One thing had been clear over the last year and especially now in the face of danger. If she ever got another chance with him, she wouldn't let it slip by like she had back in Boston. Even if that meant she'd have to seduce him, she knew she had to grab what she wanted, and she would just have to prove to him that she was what he wanted.

Slowly, so he would see, she licked her lips and lowered her eyes to watch his mouth.

"Where are we?" she whispered. In the dim light she could just see his eyes as they heated, then he blinked and pulled away, leaving her breathless.

He started pacing the small room, and then she heard him digging around in his bag. He pulled a small flashlight from one zipper. If he'd allowed her to go back for her bag, she would have her own light, and her hair brush, toothbrush, and toothpaste. She was growing more agitated by the minute, thinking of everything she'd lost.

When the small penlight hit several large brown sacks, Jason walked over and tested them by kicking them with his shoe. She heard him mumble something.

"What?" She walked over to him and stood next to him, wrapping her arms around herself.

"It's flour," he said as he turned and looked at her. "We can sleep here tonight."

"What!" she stared at him in shock. Sleep in a broom closet on bags of flour? No way! Sure, over the last year she'd roughed it in small bed and breakfasts and dingy hotel rooms. She'd even spent one night on the beach, lying under the stars. But it had been almost ninety degrees out that night and the stars and moon had been bright enough that she'd felt safe and warm. Besides, it had been only a few feet away from one of the swankiest resorts on the south of France, just outside of Nice. She'd lain there and watched the airplanes land at the small ocean-side airport and wondered where Jason was. It had been one of the best nights she could remember, but with all her travels over the last year, she never once wanted to sleep in a drafty, spider-infested broom closet while two large thugs waited somewhere outside to bag and tag her, so to speak.

"Listen, Katie..." he ran his hands through his hair, causing him to almost drop the small flashlight. "We are not going back out there tonight. Those two men will be looking everywhere, at every hotel, every bed, and break-fast, for you. We're safer staying here for the night. Then early tomorrow, we'll sneak out of town."

"So, it was them? Who are they anyway? What do they want with me?" She stood there waiting for his answers.

"I think they're after you, possibly to ransom you off to your father. I heard them talking before they jumped you and they knew your name and mentioned a ransom." He handed her the flashlight.

"Point it in the corner." He removed his jacket and as he started to move the large bags of flour around, she watched his t-shirt stretch over the muscles in his back.

She longed to know what he would feel like, to run her fingers across every tight cord. Then her eyes roamed downward and she noticed how nice his faded jeans looked stretched over his butt. She had always loved his butt and wondered how it would feel under her hands as well. He had gained a few pounds of muscle since she'd seen him last. He looked leaner, but he was more defined all over, including his backside. How would it feel to grab it and hold on as he…

Realizing where her thoughts were leading her, she shook her head and focused her eyes and the light back on his task, instead of his backside.

She watched as he made a palette of six large bags. She kicked one with her toe and watched as a small plume of smoke rose up from it. Come morning, they would both be covered in white powder.

When she looked back up, Jason had rolled his jacket up and handed it to her.

"Use it as a pillow." He took the light from her and motioned to her bed for the night.

When she just looked at him, he said, "Listen, Kat, I can see how tired you are. Just lay down and I'll take the first watch."

She crossed her arms, still waiting for answers.

"I promise I'll answer any questions you have in the morning." She could always tell when he was telling the truth and this time, she knew he meant it.

Trying to get comfortable on a pile of flour bags was no easy task. Every time she moved, white flour would smoke out from the burlap bags. By the time she settled down, she was positive she looked a lot like Casper the Friendly Ghost.

She watched as Jason folded his tall frame and sat with his back to the door, then crossed his arms over his knees.

"You aren't going to lie down?"

"No, I'll keep watch. Go ahead, get some sleep. Goodnight, Kat."

Using his jacket as a pillow, she closed her eyes and smelled his scent and flour. She trusted that he would sit there all night watching over her. Her mind kept racing with a million questions and she didn't think she would be able to fall asleep.

Then she started thinking of him, and how it had felt with his body up against hers, what it would feel like to run her hands over him, giving him and herself pleasure. Maybe she needed to step up her game and make him see that she was right for him. She wasn't opposed to stooping to seduction. She'd never tried it before, but how hard could it be? At least she knew it would be easy with him.

Jason had his back to the door and watched Katie tossing, trying to get comfortable. She'd been so soft and her smell was a memory he couldn't help but feel comfortable with. He'd actually felt aroused when her body had been pressed tight against his. He hadn't thought about Katie in that way before, at least he'd tried not to. He'd tried for years to think of her as the little sister he'd never had, but to be honest with himself, ever since they'd been roommates he had struggled with it. Watching her walk around their small apartment in nothing but a silk robe or towel, he'd had a hard time keeping the sister thought in his mind.

He had thought she didn't think about him that way,

but that kiss at the party had awakened more desires than he knew what to do with. It had been hard that night, holding still through a kiss, when all he wanted to do was lock the door and take her against it.

Then everything had been taken out of his hands. When they had met at the coffee shop, he was trying to build up enough nerve to tell her how he felt. But she just kept saying it had been a mistake, and he didn't know what to do. Then her mother had called and, well, everything had changed.

Now as he watched her sleep, something he'd done plenty of times over the years, he couldn't help but wonder why he hadn't done something about it earlier.

He remembered getting upset at several of his buddies when they'd tried to hit on her. He'd made it clear that she was off limits. Now he wondered why he'd done that if he'd had other reasons than simply protecting her like a sister like he used to think. Maybe it was his way of keeping her to himself.

He remembered the one boyfriend she'd had in college. The relationship had been short-lived, thanks to him. Ken had been a good friend, and when he'd asked Katie out, Jason had been visiting his mother in Maine that weekend. When he'd returned on Monday morning, he'd walked into their apartment to see Ken walking out of the bedroom. Katie was in the shower and Ken had a look on his face like he'd planned the whole thing for while Jason was out of town. Jason had thrown him against the wall and told him to leave and never return.

He told himself all that next month that it was for the best. Katie had been sad and upset that Ken hadn't called her back, but after a few weeks, she returned to her normal self. Ken was an okay guy, but Jason knew that he was stringing along two other girls at that time. Katie deserved better than that.

Back then, Katie had always kept her dark hair longer and she had worn the finest clothes. She'd been the type of girl who had never really left the house without looking her best. Now he looked over and noticed she didn't have a drop of makeup on, and her hair, he chuckled lightly, was coated with a dusting of flour. Her clothes looked worn and very comfortable, and he couldn't remember her looking better.

Shifting his weight and trying to get more comfortable, he remembered the one kiss he had shared with her. He remembered the softness of her lips and remembered how soft she felt just a while ago, against the wall, as he held her there. Closing his eyes, he remembered feeling her chest against his as they gasped for breath. She was small and had always felt just right in his arms. He used to chalk it up to friendship, that they had known each other forever, but he knew it was more than that.

He wondered if he had acted differently back at the party, if they would have ended up somewhere else, rather than hiding out in a storage closet, sleeping on flour bags, and running from thugs who probably wanted him dead, and Katie for ransom.

It was the only explanation he could think of and he itched to step outside and make a phone call, but he knew that Katie was a very light sleeper. He didn't want to explain who he was calling and why, so he would just have to wait until he heard the light, little snore he knew so well before sneaking out to give an update on their predicament.

If she knew that her mother was the person he'd been checking in with, he was sure she wouldn't follow him to Rome. Which was where he was sure they needed to go now that there were men after her. She needed the protection of her family and her closest family was in Rome. He didn't know Damiano and didn't want to take the chance of trusting him. He started thinking of how they'd get to Rome in the fastest way possible.

He knew she was upset at her mom. Hell, he'd been upset at her, to begin with. But things had changed when she had opened up to him one day over lunch. He'd actually sat and listened to her and he could see the changes Kathleen had made. She was different, and he couldn't deny that she'd changed for the better. So, he'd gone on this journey with her backing him the entire way. It wasn't that he needed her money; he had plenty himself. But he was going to look for Katie, anyway, and if he didn't have to touch his money while doing it, why not take the extra help. Besides, the only real cost had been hotel rooms.

Looking at Katie asleep on the pile of bags, he remembered seeing her for the first time. He had watched her walk across the hot cement around the country club's pool. She had walked towards the slide with her head held high like she owned the place. He'd been intrigued then, so he'd watched her, and seen her laugh, seen the joy she'd experienced falling down the slide. Then when she'd hit the water, he'd watched her struggle to swim to the side of the pool.

It had just been luck that he'd been watching her that day, but he still didn't know why his eight-year-old mind had locked onto her.

He still didn't know why she was the one person he

still cared more about in this world than anyone else. At first, their relationship had just been friendly. Actually, she'd annoyed him at first. He had tried everything to get rid of her at the country club. He'd begged his mom to not go every day or at least at different times. But it had never failed. Every time they drove up, she'd been standing there, waiting for him.

He remembered one time trying to go in through the back gate, just to avoid her. It was like she had a radar. She'd been there at the back gate that day, waiting. It wasn't until almost three months later, when a few other boys he'd been hanging out with made fun of her, teasing her about something, that he'd finally started looking for her each time. He didn't like having a little girl following him, but he hated bullies even more.

Two years later he realized how much she'd come to mean to him as a friend. He'd tried out for basketball in junior high; he'd made the JV team and was upset that he hadn't made varsity. When he'd gotten back to his locker, there was a small note from Katie. He still had the note tucked away in an old shoe box in his mother's attic. She'd told him how proud she'd been that he made the team, and he'd felt like a fool for not being happy about what he'd accomplished. Thirty-six other boys hadn't made the cut. She'd always grounded him like that, letting him see the things that had been truly important, instead of just the things he had thought had been important.

When he'd started looking at girls in a different way, she'd been there and never once had he thought of her in that way. He thought she'd treated him like she'd treated her brother. Looking back at it now, he could see the differences. He must have been blind to the fact that she'd held him higher than she held her brother. She'd had some-thing more for him, just like he'd always had something more for her. He'd just never had a name for the feeling.

Now he realized that she had always been more than just his best friend, she was the only person he had ever completely trusted in his entire life. He felt terrible for keeping things from her, but he knew he needed to in order to get her where he wanted her. What he was struggling with now was that where he wanted her was starting to change in his mind. He had been thinking about wanting her in places he'd never imagined before.

Shaking his head clear, he tried to close his eyes and his mind and get some rest. They were going to have a very busy day ahead of them.

CHAPTER 4

*K*atie woke when she heard the door click shut. Sitting up quickly, she coughed at the plume of flour that followed her, and then she heard Jason laugh from his seat against the front door.

"What was that?" she asked between coughs.

"What was what?" he looked across the room at her, smiling.

Looking around the room, she noticed her backpack was leaning against the opposite wall.

How? When did you go get this?" She started to grab for it.

"Hang on, Katie. Before you…" It was too late, she noticed it then. The bag had been cut open and half of the contents were missing, including her hairbrush. Rummaging through it, she took stock of everything that was missing. Her gray sweatshirt, her other pair of shoes, the hairbrush and the tube of toothpaste she'd just purchased were all gone.

She still had her shorts, another pair of jeans, and thank

goodness, all her undergarments were still accounted for. The secret money she had tucked in the inside zipper was gone. That was okay with her, it had only been fifty euro's. She had kept the means to her real money on her, just in case she ever lost her backpack.

"How did you get this back?"

"You aren't upset?"

"Upset at what? That you snuck out of here without me to retrieve my bag, or that you forced me to leave it in the first place? No."

He shook his head, "Katie, they took your passport, your wallet, everything."

She started to laugh, "Jason, I can replace my passport. Actually, I've had to once already on this trip, shortly after I arrived in England. I think I left it on the bus to Munich." She looked off in the distance trying to remember.

"Who are you and what have you done with my Katie?" When she just looked at him, he chuckled at her. "Well, I hope you're not very hungry. All I could get was a couple apples and some rolls." He pulled out a brown bag. "But we will have to eat on the road. The sun is already up and we need to make sure those men aren't around to see us leave."

Katie stood up and dusted herself off, causing such a large cloud of flour that Jason had actually stood outside waiting for it to dissipate.

She used this private time to change her shirt and finger comb her hair to look somewhat normal. Her skin felt like there was a light coat of flour all over her, and her head itched. She wanted a shower badly.

When she walked outside, the warm sun and the wonderful sounds of the town greeted her. She smelled freshly baked goods from down the street, and the town felt like it was coming alive.

She started walking towards the bus station, knowing she had only a few hours to get to the New Edges building before her meeting with the father she had never met. She still needed to stop at a clothing store and buy new clothes, then check into a hotel and shower before she met with him, so she picked up the pace as Jason walked beside her.

"Where are you going?"

"I'm heading to the bus station."

"Good idea," he said, easily matching her pace.

When they reached the bus station, she was about to walk to the counter to buy her ticket, when Jason pulled her to a stop and yanked her back out the door.

"What?" She tried to pull her arm free.

"He's here!" he hissed and continued to try to pull her away. She looked around and seeing nobody she knew, tried to pull her arm free again.

"Damn it, Katie, will you just trust me. Look." He pointed across the sidewalk, and through the glass window, she saw a large man in a dark green shirt. His nose was broken and he had a black eye. She'd never seen the man before in her life. Looking back at Jason as he continued to march them across the street, she asked.

"Is that the man who attacked me last night?"

"Yes, one of them. Hopefully, he didn't see us. Come on, we need to get out of here."

"Why don't we just…"

"No, I've got a new plan. We're getting out of town."

She stopped dead in the middle of the road. "No, I'm going to go meet my BD, across town. You can do whatever you want." She started to pull her arm free.

"Your BD?" He held onto her arm.

"Biological Dad, you know Damiano Cardone."

"Listen, Kat…" He ran his hands through his hair, looking like he was going to pull it all out. "He isn't in town anymore."

She turned to look at him. His eyes were downcast, and she would have sworn he was lying to her, but Jason had never lied to her, ever.

"How do you know that?"

"I'll answer your questions if you just follow me now; we need to get out of town quickly." He pulled her to the outskirts of town.

She stood there on a dirt road, watching him almost panic.

"We could rent a car? I think I saw…"

"No, we can't chance going back in town. There has to be --"

Just then, a large bus turned the corner and started heading towards them. Jason smiled at her and started waving his hands and walked to the middle of the road.

To say the bus was rusty was an understatement. It was packed with people, chickens, and even a few goats.

A few minutes later, she sat on the old bus in the hardest bus seat she'd ever experienced and shared her breakfast roll with the large hen which sat on her lap in an old wire cage. She smiled slowly at Jason who was sitting across from her, looking very uncomfortable.

A large Billy goat was getting a little too close to his crotch with its horns. Jason's hands kept snaking down to cup and protect himself, and Katie found this all too funny. She tried, really tried, not to laugh out loud, but the little boy who was holding the leash of the Billy goat was not paying attention and it kept putting its nose and horns where they didn't belong.

Jason had always been really good around kids. After getting his millionth black belt in Judo back in high school, he'd started teaching some of the classes himself. She'd taken his class one year and had fallen even more in love with him. He'd been so patient with her and the other kids in the class.

She'd been the only grownup in a room full of ten-year-olds and she'd enjoyed watching him interact with the younger kids. He didn't talk to them like most teenage boys did, just trying to impress a girl and acting like they were somehow very stupid. Instead, he'd talked to them like they were little adults, and he was careful to explain everything in an easy and fun manner.

She'd learned a lot that year in his class, enough to help her escape those two men last night. She knew Jason was the only reason she'd gotten away. If he hadn't been there... she shivered thinking about it.

When they had been on the bus for a little over two hours, Jason got up and walked over to her. "Come on." He nodded towards the front of the bus.

"Come on, where?"

"We're leaving." He grabbed the hen and handed the cage to a little girl who sat on the next seat, then he took Katie's hand and pulled her up. They started to make their way to the front of the crowded bus where Jason tried to communicate to the local driver. Katie leaned over and looked at the landscape just as the bus slowed down.

"We're getting off here."

"Here?" Katie looked out the window again. She didn't see any signs of a town, houses, or any other buildings. As

45

far as she could tell, there was nothing within miles of where Jason had just asked to be dropped off. They stepped off the bus, and when the doors closed, she felt a little abandoned. She watched as the bus coughed a big puff of black smoke as it left them behind.

She looked around the beautiful countryside and would have enjoyed the scenery if she wasn't worried about being stranded. The rolling hills were very green and she noticed they were full of wildflowers of almost every color. She could even smell the freshness in the air, like some of those flower plug-in's she used to buy for her bathroom.

"Well." She turned and looked at him with her arms crossed.

He smiled back at her, "Well?"

"What are we doing out here in the middle of nowhere? I walked several miles yesterday after being dropped off by a bus, and let me tell you," she stepped closer and pointed her finger into his chest, "I'm in no mood to walk that far again. We were perfectly fine on the bus; no one was following us. There was no danger. It was taking us to --" he silenced her by tugging on her hand.

"Jason!"

"It's better to show you than to stand here listening to you." He smiled at her and kept tugging her hand until she gave in and walked with him towards a small hill. She was steaming mad by the time they reached the top of the hill. What was wrong with him? He'd never talked to her like this before. Looking out over the hill, she saw that they were within a short walking distance of a small city.

"How did you know that was there? Why did we have to leave the bus?" She tugged her hand free of his, missing its warmth instantly.

"I used GPS," he said, pulling his iPhone out of his pocket. "Whoever is after you could be watching the bus routes into town. We're going to wait here until evening, then walk into town." He looked around, and after grabbing her hand again, started walking in the opposite direction.

"Stop!" She pulled her hand away and stopped walking. "I'm tired of you yanking me around by my arms." She started to cross her arms, but then realized it might look childish.

They were on top of a small hill in a very large, green field in the-middle-of-nowhere Greece, and she could see for miles as a light breeze cooled her face. Small houses with red brick tiles for roofs lined the countryside. Katie noticed that there was another small town just back down the hill from where they stood.

"Katie --"

"No! You promised me answers and I'm not going anywhere without getting some." She dropped down in the soft grass and crossed her legs. She didn't even look up at him as he hovered over her. She hadn't gotten a lot to eat that morning and the apple and the half a roll she had eaten had worn off over an hour ago. She was hot, tired, and in need of a shower and a good night's rest. She watched as several cars drove by on the road below them, not caring if anyone could see or not.

Jason sat next to her and pulled her hand into his own. "I'm sorry, Katie, for pulling you around." He tugged her hand lightly until she turned and looked at him. She could feel the tears stinging the back of her eyes and tried to blink them away.

47

He reached up and gently wiped away a tear that had started to roll down her cheek.

"Katie…"

"Don't!" she started to pull away.

"You want answers, but I need you to listen to me first."

"I know that look in your eyes. I saw it that day at the coffee shop when I explained that the kiss was just plain stupid…" she tossed her hands up, not knowing what else to say. It had been stupid back then; now, however, she wanted nothing more in the world than to kiss him again, right here, right now.

"I never did get to explain that."

"Jason, you didn't have to explain anything to me. It was written all over your face and was there in your eyes. I was drunk that night. God!" She closed her eyes and pulled her knees up to her chest, laying her forehead on them. "How many times must we go through this?" Part of her wanted to cry, knowing that he didn't think that way about her or that maybe their friendship had been ruined.

"Just once more, because you have yet to let me tell you my side of things."

Taking a deep breath, she sat up straight, looked at him, and prepared herself for the worse.

"That night at Lynda's party when you kissed me…" he started, and she held her breath and tried not to scream that they had to rehash one of the most embarrassing moments of her life over and over again.

"It's true, I was caught off guard. I hadn't thought of you, well, okay, I had, but I tried not to think of you in that way. I talked myself out of thinking of you that way. Then you were there and your lips were there…" He looked at her lips now and something shifted inside her, her stomach fluttered for reasons other than hunger. He was looking at her like she'd always wanted him to. "And I froze. My mind didn't catch up with what had happened until after you had already stormed from the room. Then that day in the cafe, I was trying to explain when you received the call from your mother and, well, I never did get a chance to explain before you left to hike around the great unknown." He was looking at his hands now and she realized she was still holding her breath.

"Jason, what exactly is it that you're saying?"

He looked at her and for the first time since she'd met him, she couldn't read what he was thinking. She'd never seen him looking so, so...what? Lost?

"I just need to try something out." He started to lean closer to her, but before he got the chance, she pulled his head down to hers and placed her mouth on his. She couldn't have stopped herself if she had tried, and she didn't want to.

For the first time since that night at the party, she understood what it must have felt like being surprised at the contact. Instead of him just sitting there, unresponsive, he was actually pulling her closer as his lips moved slowly over hers. She couldn't move, couldn't think. His hands fisted in her hair and then he moved lightly, and on a moan, she closed her eyes and let the feeling of Jason kissing her take over.

How could she not get this? He was showing her everything he'd felt for her, his entire life, all wrapped up in one kiss. He didn't want to lose her as a friend, he could never

49

lose her, it would kill him. She smelled and tasted as good as he remembered, and he wanted more of her. No, he *needed* more of her. Her hair felt so soft under his fingertips, and her skin was like silk. He ran his hand lightly down her cheek, running lower to the soft spot on her neck, then down her shoulder as he pulled her closer.

She melted against him and he heard her moan softly, almost making him lose complete control of himself. Pulling back slowly, he watched as her dark eyes focused on his face.

"I've tried not to think this way about you, tried not to want you for years." He took her mouth again, this time running his hands up and down her back as she bowed and flexed under his touch. She was soft and when he pulled her farther down to the ground, a moan escaped his lips as he trailed hot kisses down her slender neck. Her hands were fisted in his hair and he could tell she had totally lost track of where they were because she was moving under him, holding onto his hair, and the noises she was making sounded loud in the large field. He wondered what she would be like when he finally touched her, skin to skin.

My God! What would it be like when he took her? Would she scream? The thought made it almost unbearable to stop running his hands over her. But he slowly pulled away and looked down into her eyes. Her short dark hair was fanned out in the soft grass underneath them, her cheeks were the color of honey with a hint of pink, her lips… closing his eyes, he tried not to think about her lips again.

"Katie," he opened his eyes to see her watching him cautiously, "we need to have that talk." He sat up, removing himself from her soft body; he could get used to feeling it under his own.

He avoided looking at her to better control himself, and when he finally did look at her, he could see the hurt in her eyes. Putting his fingers under her chin, he pulled her face up until she looked at him.

"Don't," he said, softly. "I'm not sorry about the kiss, I actually want to do it again. But we have some things to talk about first, and I don't know about you, but I'm starving. I was going to take us down the hill to that small town and see about getting some lunch." He pointed off towards the left where she could see the small town.

"Can you wait to get your answers until after we eat?"

She nodded her head as Jason stood up and pulled her up behind him. Instead of letting her go, he pulled her into his arms and held onto her for just a minute. She smelled like flour with a hint of grass and heaven, which made him smile.

It was a short walk into the town, which sat on the side of a steep hill. The very old stone buildings were clustered within a three-block radius. each well maintained and housing their own little shops.

They quickly found the town's deli and ordered some freshly made spinach leek pie. Jason had always enjoyed trying new foods; for the most part, he hadn't found anything that he hadn't liked so far.

"Why is it that the food here is so much better than what I remember back home?" Katie said after swallowing a large mouth full of the crispy crust.

"Back home all you ever did was eat cheese pizza and drink mocha. How is your mocha addiction going, by the way?"

"Oh, I stopped drinking it except for special occasions. It took almost a month for the shakes to stop." She smiled up at him.

"Well, what do you say about having some diples pastry for dessert?"

"Oh, I love diples, as long as I can have two."

The diples were the best he'd ever had; the large honey roll was still warm and tasted like heaven. Katie enjoyed them so much, she tried to steal several bites of his. He swatted her hands away lightly, laughing at her face as she pouted.

He had been impressed when she had spoken Greek and placed their order to the older women behind the counter. He'd been in the country less than a month and had only picked up some basic words. She must have guessed his thoughts from the way he was looking at her.

"So, I bought a translation book. It's not like I expect everyone to speak English." He'd actually found out that a lot of people did speak English everywhere he'd gone. So far, he'd only had to learn a handful of useful words in French, Spanish, Italian, and Greek.

Sometimes Katie was the same old Katie he'd known forever. Other times he saw that the last year had done something to her, changed her. He would see her eyes cloud over and she'd become distant, and he could see the sadness overcoming her. He understood the betrayal she'd suffered; it's not everyone that finds out their mother was married to someone else while they were married to your father. To be hit double with the knowledge that the man who'd raised you wasn't actually your biological father, Jason had seen firsthand what it had done to her.

After she found out via the phone call from her mother, she'd passed out cold on the floor of the coffee shop.

Once she'd woken, thanks to some smelling salts from an emergency kit in the bakery, he'd driven her home. She had looked like a ghost and hadn't said a word during the short drive. Her eyes seemed hollowed out, her skin, which was normally a light tan, had been pale and clammy. He'd hated seeing her that way. Less than a month later, she'd taken off and left the country.

He knew it was in part due to her friends turning on her. Even he had felt betrayed by some of the things everyone else had said about Katie and his relationship, none of it true at the time.

Now, as she excused herself and headed to the back of the place towards the bathrooms, he watched the busy room to make sure no one watched them. He'd been cautious walking into town, and he figured the place was small enough that he could spot anyone who appeared out of place.

Taking this moment, he pulled out his cell phone and decided instead of a lengthy call he would just text his message instead.

– *Made contact – someone tried to grab her – she's safe*

– *Where are you?*

– *Just outside Patra – change of plans, coming to you – taking a plane tomorrow – should be there soon*

– *Be careful*

He tucked his phone back into his jeans and waited for Katie to come back out of the restroom.

❄

"I told you they'd be trying to make it back here." The accent was so thick; it was hard for him to make out what the voice was saying over the disposable phone he'd been given. "They are in Patra, heading to the airport. Find them. I don't have to tell you how important it is that she doesn't make it here."

The man rolled his eyes and squinted in pain when he remembered the black eye and broken nose he'd received the night before. He'd been hearing how important it was that Katie Derby didn't make it to Rome ever since he'd been hired two weeks ago. So far, the only chance he'd gotten to grab the girl had ended badly and now he had a broken nose and two chipped teeth to show for it.

"I know where she is, and I told you I'd get her. She's with a man and he knows how to fight. It may end up costing you double because of him, and I might have to hire a couple more guys."

"Do what you must, just stop her from getting to Rome."

He heard a click and felt like tossing the small phone through the window of the moving car. He knew how to do his job, and he'd be damned if he would sit by and let some little girl slip through his fingers, especially considering the amount of money he was about to make. He looked over at his partner and saw the large lump on his forehead that he'd received last night. He'd been doing jobs like this his whole life and knew who he could trust and who he couldn't. Watching his partner, he knew the man was one that he trusted completely. They'd been working together since they'd been kids.

"Raul, they're in Patra. I told you that tracking device would come in handy." He watched the small screen of the device that was showing him exactly where Katie Derby was. "Damn thing is not very reliable, keeps cutting out."

"I told you we should have bought the more expensive one," Raul said.

Maybe he was right, but he didn't want to explain that he'd blown through most of the advance they'd gotten for the job. After all, the van hadn't been cheap, and they still had a lot of traveling to do, so he'd set some money aside for his expenses. Now he thought he'd have to hire a few other guys to help watch the ports, maybe send them ahead to Rome. He still had a few other methods of getting his hands on the girl again; he'd be damned if he let her slip through his fingers next time.

$\mathcal{R}$ic Derby sat in the office at his art gallery, The Blue Spot, in Portland, Oregon and stared at the clock. His one o'clock appointment hadn't lasted long enough, leaving him with over an hour to kill before his next appointment. An appointment he'd been waiting for his whole life.

One little pink stick had said "yes", so he was pretty sure the answer was yes, but his new wife of just under a year hadn't trusted it. So he'd had to go down to the corner store, just before midnight, where he had bought one of every kind of pregnancy test. Still, Roberta hadn't believed those either, hence their doctor appointment at four today.

He was so nervous, it was like he was back in college taking a test, and he prayed to God that he would pass this one. They hadn't planned on getting pregnant this soon, but neither of them could be happier or more nervous. Ever since Roberta had retired from the Portland Police Department as Detective, she'd been head of security for their art galleries. He enjoyed working with her and loved spending time with her every day.

When the phone rang, he was almost too engrossed in his thoughts to register the sound.

"Blue Spot Galleries."

The voice was computerized and almost too low to hear. "If you ever want to see your sister, Katie Derby, alive again, you will wire ten million dollars to the offshore account by this time tomorrow." Ric rushed to write down the bank information that was said and repeated quickly.

There was a click and Ric felt like passing out. It took him less than five seconds to pick up the phone and dial it again.

"Dad, someone's…"

"I received a call, too, son. Not two minutes ago."

Just then Roberta, Ric's wife walked in. "Hang on, Dad. Rob's here." He punched the speakerphone button as Roberta looked at him with a questioning look.

After filling his wife in on what was happening, he watched her put on her "cop mask" and take charge of the call as she got to work. When they hung up with his father ten minutes later, she had the FBI on the phone and was relaying every detail of the calls.

Rodrick had updated them on Katie's last whereabouts. She'd been in Greece the last time he'd heard. They had decided the best thing to do was work with Damiano and Dante in Italy to track down the trail.

Fifty minutes later, Ric and his father had chartered a plane to Rome. Roberta would stay behind and work with the FBI while waiting for any other calls.

Three hours later, Ric and Rodrick were both sitting on

his private jet, watching the ground disappear beneath them. Rushing to find Katie had been something both of them had demanded to take part in.

Something wasn't right. Jason had been waiting too long for Katie to come back out of the restroom. Grabbing his bag, he headed to the back and banged on the woman's restroom door. When no one answered, he tried the door handle. Jerking it open, he was shocked to see Katie in a small white tank top and tight little shorts. She had her head in the sink, and her face and hair were under the fast stream of water coming from the faucet. She was lathering up her hair with shampoo and he noticed bubbles running down her bare neck and arms.

When he'd barged in, she'd jerked her head up, slamming it on the corner of the sharp metal faucet.

"Ouch, damn it, Jason!" She rubbed her head with her fingers, near the spot she'd just hit.

Recovering, he quickly shut the door behind him, locked them in, and walked over to her. He dropped his bag next to hers then took her head in his hands and looked at the small injury.

She was still bent over the sink, her wet hair dripping in her eyes and face. "Here, let me see. Oh, man. You've got a small cut here. The faucet must have been sharp."

"Can't I just have a few minutes to clean up without having you barge in here acting like you're a white knight trying to rescue me?" He could see tears of pain in her eyes as she looked up at him. Then again, he thought, maybe they were from the shampoo dripping into her eyes.

"Shh." He pulled her head back towards the sink. "Here, let me help." He started splashing water over her soapy head.

She braced her hands on the sink ledge and held on. He could see her shifting her feet to bend over and knew that the position was probably uncomfortable for her.

"There was so much flour in my hair, I just had to clean some of it out," she said over her shoulder while trying to look at him.

He turned her head back and placed it over the sink, then he cupped his hands, scooping the water up and gently dumping it over her hair, washing the bubbles from it.

She became very still while holding onto the side of the sink for support, so he continued rinsing her hair until it was clean. When he was done, he bent over and picked up the small hand towel she'd dropped.

He turned her around, so she faced the mirror and slowly rubbed her hair dry. He leaned her head down so he could gently part her hair where the small cut was. He noticed the bleeding had stopped thanks to the cold water, but he still made sure it was clean before continuing to dry her hair.

He wiped the water from her shoulders and arms and his eyes roamed over her in the mirror. He noticed that her face was pink and looked flushed. Then he saw that her white tank top had gotten a little wet from leaning over the sink. He could just make out dark circles through the wet material and enjoyed seeing her nipples poking upward, thanks to the cold water.

He became painfully hard as he stood behind her. Looking up into her face, he noticed that she was now watching him in the mirror. She had a look on her face like she'd never seen him before.

"What?" She sounded breathless.

"What? What?" he almost whispered in response.

She watched him in the mirror, and it took all his willpower not to look at her nipples through the wet shirt again.

"Why are you looking at me like that?" she asked.

"Like what?" He tried to stop thinking about her, about wanting to see all of her.

Her hair had been so soft under his hands and he had thoroughly enjoyed washing it; there was something so intimate about the simple act. In the small room, he could smell her shampoo, a sexy scent with a hint of honey, just like her.

The room seemed to be getting smaller, and he licked his lips and watched as she started to finger comb her hair.

He bent down and reached into his bag and pulled out a small comb, then watched her face in the mirror as he started to gently pull it through her hair.

He enjoyed seeing her eyes close in pleasure as he kept running it through her hair, making sure to gently work out any tangles. She leaned back against him, and he thought she would feel what she was doing to him since he was pressed right up against her tight little butt. If she moved just a little against him, he was sure he would explode right then and there.

When her hair was combed smooth, he set the comb down on the counter-top and she opened her eyes to look at him in the mirror. He could see the passion and maybe a hint of something else there. Determination?

With his eyes on her, he leaned down and placed a soft

kiss on her neck, just below her ear. Her eyes closed again, and she moaned with delight, leaning her head back against him. His hands roamed up and down her arms, spreading small bumps along her skin. He licked the underside of her ear and dipped his tongue in, just for a taste. He slowly nibbled on her earlobe and swore he heard her purr.

Her body was pressed tight against his and when he moved his hands to her front, he pulled her back tighter against his desire. Her eyes flew open quickly and then she smiled at him in the mirror. He just smiled back and continued his kisses along her jawline until she relaxed back against him. He watched in the mirror as he slowly moved his hands up until he cupped her perfect breasts with his hands and felt her tight nipples peak against his fingers. He rolled them lightly between his fingers and enjoyed seeing her eyes cloud as she leaned her head back against him, totally losing control.

He moved one hand slowly down her flat stomach until it rested at the top of her shorts. When she didn't push him away, he dipped his hand between her skin and the denim, feeling her soft skin, playing his fingers over the soft hair that covered her below. Using just his finger, he roamed farther down until he found her hot and wet. He parted her soft folds and pushed a finger into her slowly. Her hips stopped moving and she closed her eyes and rested her head on his shoulder with a moan.

He slid his finger in and out a few times, slowly. He could feel her slickness and wished he could see all of her, taste her, smell her, and lap her up.

Then he rubbed his finger over her again and felt her

hips moving slowly with his movement, gliding his finger farther.

He wanted to yank her tight shorts down quickly, then bend her over and bury himself in her sweet wetness.

She was riding his finger and he could tell that she was on the verge of coming when there was a light knock on the door. Her eyes flew open and as she looked at him in the mirror, he watched realization flood her face, and her cheeks turned a bright shade of red.

Removing his hand slowly, he kissed her neck and said against her skin, "We'd better be going. It's getting late and we have a lot of walking to do." He bent to get his bag, trying to shake the image of Katie, wet, hot, and on the verge of coming in his hand, out of his mind.

Three hours later as the sun was beginning to sink lower, his mind was on anything but Katie in a wet shirt and tight, little shorts.

"Can you complain anymore?" he asked over his shoulder.

"You said we were just outside of town. You didn't say we weren't going to stop in that town. Why are we still walking? Why haven't we stopped?" She reached over and yanked on his arm until he spun around and looked at her. Her hair had dried in the sun, leaving it curly. Sweat was rolling down her neck and face and he could see she wasn't going to take another step until he answered at least one of her questions.

"We haven't stopped yet, because we are not where we are heading." He tried to turn around.

"Jason Allen Keaton!" She stomped her foot and looked at him like his mother used to. It didn't have the same effect. "Where are we heading?"

"Rome." He started to turn around again.

"Oh no! If you think I'm going to walk to Rome, you'd better think again." She walked over to the side of the road and sat down in the dirt. Then she removed her left shoe and started shaking it until a few pebbles dropped out.

"We are not walking to Rome." He laughed and rolled his eyes. He wanted to tell her about the large body of water that sat between them and Italy, but instead, he said, "We're walking to Patra to catch a plane to Brindisi, then maybe hop a bus or train to Rome. And we're going to miss the flight today if you don't get your butt out of the dirt and back on the road."

Katie's mind snapped. "I am NOT going to Rome! I know who's in Rome, I'm not stupid you know." She threw her shoe at him. He ducked, but it barely missed his head. She walked over to him and pointed her finger into his chest. "Is this what it comes down to? Loyalties! Me or her, Jason. Choose." She was so close to his face, her eyes shot metaphorical daggers at him, and he could feel the heat vibrating off her.

"Katie…" What could he say? He hadn't planned on the words, how he would tell her. "We're heading to Rome because your father is there." That's it, lie to her, Jason. That will get her moving.

"What? No, he isn't. Damiano Cardone is in Athens. I should know, since I was supposed to have a meeting with him today, remember."

She walked over and picked up the shoe she had thrown at him and put it back on her foot after dusting off her sock.

"Well, he's there now. I told you he wasn't in Athens anymore." He continued walking.

64

She hurried up and grabbed her bag again, jogging to catch up with him.

"I won't see her, you know."

"I know, Katie. I think she knows it as well." He put his arm around her shoulder as they walked towards town.

"I don't think I can ever see her again. How can you forgive someone who spent your whole life lying to you?"

He stopped and pulled her shoulders until she looked at him.

"She might have her own reasons for doing what she did. Until you hear her side of things, you need to try to keep an open mind."

"I can't, Jason. I just can't."

"You judged me without hearing my side of the story."

She tilted her head in question.

"About the kiss. You had assumed that I didn't think about you in that way, but upon hearing my side of things, I hope you understand how I feel about you now."

He could see understanding in her eyes now and a little excitement.

"What if she doesn't have a reason for doing what she did? What if she is just some big slut who likes to sleep around and hurt people?"

"Katie, I think you know her a little better than that. Plus, you heard they got married right?"

"Yes." She dropped her head and started looking at their shoes. "But, that doesn't change anything."

"Why not? If Damiano was forgiving enough to marry her, the woman who had lied to him all this time, maybe you should be as open-minded."

"I don't think I can. Please," she tried to pull away. "I don't want to talk about this anymore.

He watched as she turned and started walking again. They walked in silence the rest of the way.

They made it into Patra just after the sun had set and stopped at the first hotel they found, where they got a small room with two large beds.

Katie stood in the shower and let the water wash away the day's dirt and sweat. She tried not to think about their discussion earlier. Instead, she chose to think about their relationship.

She'd always been jealous of Jason's girlfriends, but one had always stood out more than the others. Kimberly had been a thorn in Katie's side. The busty redhead had Jason wrapped around her finger for almost a year. He'd started dating her shortly after Katie had moved into the two-bedroom apartment with him. She'd been trying to help him out with rent and, to be honest with herself, she'd been hoping the close proximity would spark some interest in her.

Instead, he'd started dating Kimberly. Katie remembered the first time they'd been left alone in the room together.

"I know that you have a crush on my boyfriend." Kimberly hadn't even looked at her.

They'd been sitting in the living room, getting ready to watch a movie. Jason had excused himself to go make the popcorn.

"I'm sorry?" Katie had been shocked by the girl's tone.

"Don't play coy with me." She turned her body and

Katie got the full view of her size D breasts popping out of her tight pink shirt. "I know you have a crush on Jason. I don't like that you live with him and I will do everything in my power while I'm with him to get him to change his mind about your living arrangements."

Katie had almost wanted to laugh. Jason and Kimberly had been dating for less than two months at that point. For this redheaded bimbo to think that her Jason would choose this girl over their friendship was laughable.

But when Jason had walked back in with a large bowl of popcorn, Kimberly had stood up and faked a cry.

"Really, Jason. I don't know how you can live with this girl." Jason almost dropped the bowl of popcorn. He'd looked between the pair and then back at Kimberly. Katie just watched Kimberly with amusement.

"I want to go home. I won't be insulted like this. Especially by someone like her." She had pointed at Katie, and then Katie watched in horror as Jason rushed over and set the bowl of popcorn down and hugged Kimberly.

"I'm sorry, did Katie say something to upset you?"

Jason gave her his best stink-eye behind Kimberly's back. Katie just looked like she wanted to laugh. He saw the look and immediately knew Kimberly was lying.

"I'll take you home." As he was walking the bimbo out, he looked back over his shoulder and mouthed, 'I'm sorry,' to Katie.

Every time Kimberly was around, Jason tried to keep them apart. It had only taken six more months for Katie to tire of the game and move out.

To be honest with herself, it was the loud noises that came from Jason's room at night that had finally made her decide to move out. She knew that Kimberly probably did it on purpose, but she just couldn't spend another night crying as he made love to her.

Then Katie started thinking about what had happened at lunch today in the woman's restroom. How Jason's hands had moved her to somewhere that had always been just out of reach. She was sure she'd sounded a lot like Kimberly had. Her nipples hardened as she remembered his mouth on her neck and his fingers pinching her nipples lightly, rolling them between his fingers.

She ran her soapy hands over her body and wished they were his, remembering how good his callused hands felt running over her soft skin. She ran her fingers over herself, seeing if it felt as good as it had with his. It didn't feel the same, but still, she tried to remember his fingers running over her and mimicked his movements.

She tried very hard to relax and not think of how stupid she felt standing in the shower touching herself, but her mind just wouldn't shut off. Finally, she rinsed herself off, realizing that she would probably remain so wound up that she would explode when he touched her next.

She smiled when she realized she was counting on him touching her again, not saying if, but when. She thought of several ways she could convince him to touch her again; she knew she was up for the challenge. When she walked out, wearing only her shorts and a clean tank top, Jason was on the phone. When he saw her, he quickly clicked the phone off and watched her cross the room. Without saying anything, he shook his head and walked into the restroom, closing the door behind him. She almost stomped her foot in frustration. She had seen the desire flash in his eyes and wondered what it would take for it to be there again.

Sitting down on the side of the bed, she decided to

order room service and, because she was very hungry, she ordered almost everything on the menu. Watching television did little to entertain her since everything was in Greek and very hard to follow, so she turned it off and waited for Jason to get out of the shower or for the food to get there.

She thought about his phone conversation; of course, she knew who he'd been talking to. It was obvious, and she didn't know why he didn't just come out and say it. Maybe he was afraid of how she would react?

There was a light knock on the hotel door and then the bathroom door swung open quickly. Jason walked out of the bathroom, the small white towel hung low on his hips. He had a razor in one hand and she noticed that half of his face was shaved, while the other half was still covered in shaving cream. He walked over to the door and peeked out the peephole, then turned to her, "Did you order food?"

"Yes, of course, I did." She tried to move him aside, so she could open the door.

"Get back, just there." He pointed behind the bathroom door. Shrugging her shoulders, she moved to where he told her. She figured if it got her the food, she'd pretty much do anything at this point.

Finally, after he rolled the cart of food in himself, he shut himself back up in the bathroom to finish shaving. She sat down and started eating her feast while sitting on the bed. Halfway through her chicken ravioli, he came back out wearing gray shorts and a clean white t-shirt. His hair was slicked back, and he looked fresher with his shaved face.

"I ordered you a steak and some pasta." She nodded towards a covered plate.

They sat in silence as they ate, and she felt like there was some unspoken tension building. She could feel his nerves build and felt her desire triple.

"What?" she finally asked after catching him staring at her again.

"What?" He didn't even try to hide the humor this time, and she laughed with him.

"I'm sorry about today," he said quietly.

Instantly her mind flashed to what he'd done to her in the restroom.

"No, God, Katie, not that," She watched him shake his head. "I'm sorry you had to walk so much. I know my feet hurt. I didn't know it was that far, I swear."

"It's okay, it's not like a ten-mile walk is going to kill me."

"Well, it was more like fifteen, but if you want to call it ten, I can live with that." He smiled and set his empty plate down, then watched her. She had just finished her plate of ravioli and had uncovered her desert, which she had ordered with him in mind.

She took the plate with her to the bed and sat down, leaning back against the headboard. She picked up a juicy strawberry and dipped it slowly in the cream, then using just two fingers, she brought the berry to her lips and sucked the cream off it slowly. She heard Jason catch his breath from across the room.

"What?" She looked at him, smiling.

"You ordered strawberries and cool whip for dessert?" he leaned towards her.

"Yes." She looked at him and noticed his eyes were a deeper blue than she could ever remember. They roamed over her shirt and she felt her nipples harden. Jason noticed and grinned at her, causing her to get wet between her legs. When did he get the power to do this to her? She had planned on seducing him, how could she have known that he would do the same to her?

"Come over here and I'll give you a taste," she said, then watched as he got off his chair and started walking towards her slowly.

When he reached the side of the bed, she dipped her finger in the cool whip, then held her finger up for him to lick the cream off. He looked into her eyes and she knew she had won this battle; she could see him submitting to his desire. He sat on the edge of the bed and leaned closer, then he took her finger into his mouth and sucked lightly. She closed her eyes on a moan. She couldn't move.

After her finger was cleaned, she watched him dip his finger into the cool whip and swirl it around slowly. Then he moved his finger to her mouth and waited as she opened her lips and took the cream covered digit into her mouth and slowly sucked the sweet cream off his finger. She watched as his eyes darkened and thought she heard him moan when her tongue rolled around his finger.

"Katie…" He watched as she took a strawberry and dipped it in the cream, then brought it to his mouth for him to enjoy. He slowly rolled his tongue over it, licking the cream off until he nibbled on the plump berry, sucking the juice from her fingers.

He gave her a wicked smile and dipped a berry in the cream, but instead of bringing it to her mouth, he ran it over her bare shoulder, then ran his mouth over the trail of cream and berry juice it left on her skin. She closed her eyes and enjoyed the feel of his mouth on her heated skin.

He pulled the thin strap of her tank-top down her

shoulder and continued to run the creamy berry down over her tight nipple, running it around the bud. He dipped his head and licked every drop of juice off her. She'd never experienced anything so exciting before, and she was sure she was about to explode.

He repeated the movements on her other nipple after pulling her shirt up, exposing her stomach and her entire chest to his view. She had always enjoyed the curves she had inherited from her mother and had known guys had looked at her chest, but none had ever run their hot mouths over it like Jason was doing now.

After he'd enjoyed cleaning both nipples off, he laid her back on the bed and removed her shirt slowly. She nervously watched as he took another berry with cream and ran a trail down between her breasts, down her flat stomach, swirling it once around her belly button, stopping just above her shorts. He held the berry over her mouth until she bit into it and licked the juices off her lips. Then he dipped his head between her breasts, licking and sucking the trail, down her body until he dipped his tongue into her bellybutton, which almost caused her to jump off the mattress in excitement.

Her hands went into his wet hair and she held him as he licked the trail to the top of her shorts. He lightly pulled her shorts down until she was naked, lying on the bed for him to view every inch of her. She felt herself quivering in anticipation, wanting him to touch her, to taste her.

He reached over and took another berry and this time ran it lightly over her pink lips. She closed her eyes and felt him touching her for the second time that day, where no one had ever touched her before. The wet, slick juices rolled down her and she held still in anticipation, then she heard him moan.

"So beautiful," he said just before he nibbled on her lips and ran his tongue up and down where he had been rolling the berry around just a second before. Her hands were in his hair and she couldn't help holding on as he used his mouth against her core. He pulled back and she watched as he leaned over and dipped his fingers into the white cream. Moving back to her, he dipped one, then another finger into her and her shoulders came off the bed. He placed a hand flat on her stomach to hold her still and watched her face as he rubbed the cream over her slowly until finally, he dipped his head to lick the sweetness from her. Using his fingers and tongue, he sucked her until finally, she felt herself building to a release.

"Let go, Kat, just let go," he moaned against her skin.

When she screamed his name, he lapped her up like she had been the best dessert.

"Mmm, have I ever told you that cream and strawberries are my favorite dessert?" he chuckled against her neck a few minutes later.

She smiled, knowing it was his one weakness and thought it had just become her favorite as well.

He had moved back up to her and covered them both with the blanket. Now he was snuggling against her neck as she lay there naked, quivering with pleasure.

"Jason?"

"Shh, we have plenty of time. I know you must be tired; I know I am." She held still for a while thinking that he was just pacifying her, but when she heard him starting to snore, she realized he'd been just as worn out as she

73

was. Closing her eyes, she quickly fell asleep, naked in a man's arms and she didn't even care.

"They are going to be at the airport in the morning. I want some men in Rome watching the airport there just to make sure they don't slip by you."

"You don't have to tell me how to do my job."

"Apparently I do. Don't forget, if you don't deliver her, you won't see a dime of the rest of the money. I want her there, unharmed and on time. It's very important."

"I understand, and you'll have her there on time. Now let me do my job." He hung up with a quick snap of the phone.

"I'm tired of being told how to do my job. Raul, we've been doing this job for years, not once have we ever been told what to do. I don't like it. Maybe this time we took off more than we can bite, eh?"

"Chew. It's maybe we took off more than we can chew. I thinks."

The two friends laughed. "Come on, my friend, let's go get our prize."

Katie woke in the dark, in a sweat. She didn't know what had caused her to wake at this hour but looking around the dark room she realized someone was in the room with them. She could hear them moving around softly, and she thought she saw movement over in the corner, but out of fear she didn't move or speak. She just stared into the darkness, waiting for something to happen. It was too dark to see, but she knew someone was there, just out of sight.

She tried to move her hand to wake Jason, but she was frozen, she couldn't even squeeze his arm. When she tried to open her mouth to scream for him, nothing came out. She felt like a fish out of water, her mouth opening and closing widely several times.

Her arms wouldn't move, nothing would work, and she watched in horror as a large man with no teeth came slowly out of the darkness towards her. His hands were stretched out and she saw a pair of shiny handcuffs in one of his thick hands and a dirty potato bag in the other.

She tried to jump up, to scream, anything…

"Katie! Katie!" Jason screamed over and over again, shaking her until she finally woke from the nightmare.

He reached over and flipped on the light. Freed from her paralysis, she frantically looked around the room. No one was hiding in the shadows, no one was there except for them.

"Are you okay, Kat?" He moved to take her into his arms.

"Yeah, I think… It was just a dream," she said, more to assure herself than anything.

"It's okay, you're okay." He ran his hands down her hair and held her in a tight hug.

She noticed the room was getting lighter and hated knowing she'd started the day this way. But then she realized she was in Jason's arms and closed her eyes to the warm feeling of him holding her.

"We'd better get going. Our flight leaves in a few hours," he said into her hair. She looked over at the clock and realized it was just past seven. Their flight left at ten, which gave them just enough time to dress, eat, and make it to the airport.

Just then the hotel phone rang. "That's our wake-up call." He leaned over and answered it.

Katie wrapped the sheet around her as she hunted for her clothes, which had ended up all over the floor; for once, she hadn't cared about the mess.

A few hours later, after eating some fresh blueberry muffins from a local bakery down the street, they made it to the small airport.

People came and went, and she was actually excited to get out of Greece. Maybe she was looking forward to the change of scenery or just the possibility of getting away from trouble. Still, Jason stopped her from walking straight to the ticket booth to check in. He told her to hold back, just out of sight for a while. So they stood against the wall and watched people come and go for a few minutes. Then he cussed under his breath.

"What?"

"Hang on," he said, pulling her back further.

"Why?"

"Katie are you going to question me the entire trip?"

"Maybe."

He rolled his eyes at her, then said, "There, do they look familiar?"

She looked over at the large group of people he was pointing at, all of them over fifty and wearing matching shirts; they looked like they were part of a bowling team. "Who?"

"Those two men, standing to the left of the group."

"No, why?"

"Look again!"

She did, and she noticed that the two men didn't have the bowling shirts on and one of them had a broken nose and a black eye. The other one was walking with a slight limp.

"Are those the –"

"Yes, damn it."

"What are we going to do? They're standing at the entrance. How are we going to get tickets?"

Then Jason turned and shoved her back and took her mouth with his. He angled his body so the only thing anyone would see if they looked, was a young couple kissing.

He kept her pinned against the stone wall until she was out of breath, then finally and quickly he released her mouth, leaving her dizzy.

"Damn it to hell."

"Well, I'm so sorry that didn't meet with your satisfaction." She tried to push him away a little.

"No, not that, there are five of them now." He glanced over his shoulder. "Damn it."

"Really, Jason, we're going to have to do something about your language. How do you know there are five of them?" She tried to look over his shoulder.

"Because they are all talking to each other. Take a look underneath my arm." She did as he asked and watched the five men talking. It appeared to her that they were arguing with the large guy with the broken nose. The three new men looked like brothers; they had matching dark hair, faces, and builds. They looked like farmers, dressed in rugged pants and blue work shirts, and they were covered in either grease or dirt.

Then the three new men broke off and started walking towards the ticket booths.

"Three of them are buying tickets," she said as she kept her eyes glued to the other two.

"Damn it!" She chanced a glance at Jason's face and realized he was watching her closely. Turning her eyes back to the two original men, she watched as they each broke off.

"Quick, one's coming this way."

He grabbed her arm so fast, she thought she heard a slight pop. Then they were sprinting out of the airport and down a street, running past the crowded shops and tourists.

She was out of breath when he finally stopped several blocks later, just on the outskirts of town.

"What now?"

"Shh." He pulled her closer, back into the darkness of a doorway. She couldn't hear anything but herself breathing heavily.

"What?" She whispered.

"I don't hear anything."

"Neither do I."

"Good."

"Great!" Neither of them moved. His eyes darted down to her mouth and she remembered the feel of his lips there. Why was she thinking about him in this way while they were in danger? Her heart skipped, and she could feel her pulse vibrating under his view as his eyes wandered down her neck.

Then a young boy rolled by on a bike that was much too big for him and they jumped apart quickly, looking at each other like they had been caught stealing candy.

Jason turned and started to pull her along the road

again. They ate up the ground quickly, putting as much distance between them and the airport as they could.

"How are we going to get to Rome now?" she asked as they walked past rows of houses.

"There's always a ferry," he said, looking over at her.

"A ferry? Does it leave from around here?"

"No, it connects through Igoumenitsa."

"How do you know that?"

He tapped his head, "Great memory. I studied the ferry schedule while you were shampooing your hair."

"Well, how do we get to Igoumenitsa?"

He stopped and looked around, thinking. She stood there and watched people come and go in a small market area. She noticed a sign and knew just enough to understand what it said.

"How about we rent a scooter?" she said, pointing to a large sign. Underneath it sat a half-dozen scooters in different bright colors.

He looked over his shoulder, then looked back at her and smiled.

As it turned out, they could only take the scooters halfway to Igoumenitsa. They had to be returned in a small town there, no later than that evening. But it would get them out of town and halfway to their destination, which was about four hours away in a car that could travel at normal speeds. The scooter's top speed was thirty-five.

"Why don't we just rent a car?" she asked, thinking about the long trip ahead of them.

"Where is your sense of adventure?" he asked, smiling at her. "Besides, this was your idea, remember?"

They ended up having to also purchase shatterproof sunglasses after the scooter guy informed them in broken

English that it was required on all motorbikes. Katie had a bright purple helmet and Jason's was red. She thought he looked even more handsome in the funny looking helmet which made his head look as big as ET's.

When she told him this as they were getting on the bike, he just laughed and asked her if she had looked at herself lately. She bent over and, seeing herself in the side mirror, realized her helmet appeared three times bigger than her head.

Jason drove, and she held on to him as they made their way slowly out of Petra. They headed towards the mouth of the gulf and the large bridge that she'd seen yesterday, hovering over the canal. The massive, white bridge hung in the air, supported by hundreds of large, thick cables. She wasn't normally afraid of crossing bridges, but on the scooter, she felt more exposed. Tucking her head into Jason's back, she closed her eyes for most of the two-mile trip across the Gulf's choppy waters. She let out a large sigh of relief when they hit the other side. Looking over her shoulder, she could admire the beauty of the bridge, now that she was no longer under the large cables and over the cold, dark waters.

They took their time traveling over the hilly landscape on the wide highway as cars zipped by them quickly. The traffic lessened once they hit the side highway and Katie could finally sit back and enjoy the weather. It was warm, and the breeze felt wonderful on her face. Jason had stuffed their backpacks into the side compartments on the scooter, so when she leaned close and held onto him, there was nothing between them. She enjoyed molding her body against his and marveled at the feel of his tight stomach against her hands as she held on. She could feel his body rise and fall with his breathing and wanted to stay in this position forever.

At one point she brazenly explored the muscles along his stomach and chest. He pulled over and turned to look at her.

"If you keep doing that, I'm going to crash." He tried to lean over and kiss her, but their large helmets clanked together, and they both laughed.

Another hour later and her butt cheeks had gone numb, and she couldn't feel her toes or her hands.

"Can we stop soon?" she said over the roar of the other cars, passing them quickly.

"How about lunch?"

They stopped in the small town of Stanos and enjoyed a very small, local cafe. The food always seemed so much better in some of the "off the map" places.

The gyros were some of the best she'd had so far, the meat juicy, with just the right amount of spices. They actually watched the man make fresh pita bread in front of them as they waited. Then he'd carved the lamb meat off a large spit which held the chunk of meat over the flame. The grilled onions and peppers were caramelized to perfection.

They sat in the cafe, enjoying the locals and food for almost an hour, then hit the road again. Katie groaned when she sat back down on the seat. Her butt hadn't quite recovered yet, and she was sure that by the time they got to where they were going, it would be bruised.

It took them another three hours at the scooter's maximum speed to get where they were going. They had almost an hour before sunset after turning the scooter and their ET helmets back in. They started walking the streets of Ioannina, a large town on the shores of a large lake. There were several other towns around it, making it feel more like a large city than individual towns. As they looked for someplace to stay for the night, she realized how badly her butt and legs hurt from the day spent on the back seat of the scooter. She'd stretched as much as she could, but she was still sore from sitting in the same spot for too long.

They walked along uneven stone roads. After she'd stumbled for the third time, Katie wondered how Jason wasn't tripping all over the ground.

"Pick your feet up, Katie." He grabbed to steady her.

"I'm trying!" He stopped, and she could tell that he was looking at her.

"Come on, I think there is someplace we can stay just down here."

"Not another flour closet," she smiled. "I refuse to sleep on sacks of anything." He chuckled.

"No, I think I see a bed and breakfast sign.

An hour and a hundred dollars later, Katie sank down under the lukewarm water in the bathtub and realized how wonderful it felt not to be walking, riding a scooter, or traveling anymore that day. Her muscles slowly relaxed under the warm water and she closed her eyes.

The room was small and they were going to have to share a bed. She smiled at that and was happy she was going to sleep in a soft bed again tonight. What could be better?

Then her mind wandered to what Jason had done to her last night. Her cheeks heated and she started questioning if he had gotten any pleasure from it. She didn't know much about what guys wanted, but her friends had always talked about their boyfriends around her like she had known like she had experienced everything they had. She had always kept quiet when they talked about their sex lives, and she had never once let on that she was not only inexperienced but still a virgin. She'd always kept herself for one man, and he was sitting in the next room, waiting for her to get out of the bath. She thought about what he had done last night and knew she needed to take matters into her own hands to please him in the same manner tonight.

Less than half an hour later, she walked out of the bathroom wrapped in a large towel and found a small cart with silver plates sitting in the middle of the room with the most wonderful smells coming from it. She lifted a lid and saw a large square of pasta covered with some kind of breading. Dipping her finger in it, she tasted and closed her eyes to the richness.

She heard a noise and opened her eyes to see Jason staring at her again.

"What?"

"What? What?"

"Are we really going to keep doing this?" She set the lid back down, keeping the food warm.

Then he smiled quickly and said, "They didn't have strawberries and cream." He shook his head in disappointment and walked into the bathroom without another word, as she blushed to the roots of her hair.

Quickly getting dressed in her light shorts and t-shirt, Katie sat back down in front of the television to watch the news as she ate her dinner.

Less than ten minutes later, Jason walked back into the room. He was dripping wet with a dark pair of boxers on and was using the towel to dry his hair. She'd seen him like this a million times; after all, they'd been roommates once. He hadn't made a point of walking around in boxers in front of her, but she'd always found an excuse to be in his room when he'd come out of the shower. But seeing him like this after what they had done was different.

His sandy hair was pushed back away from his face, the water making it look darker than it was. He hadn't shaved, so he had a full day's growth going, which only gave him a more dangerous look. She'd always admired his muscles. He had taken years of Judo and she loved the way they rippled down his stomach. He didn't have much hair on his chest and she found that very sexy. She wondered if he would be as smooth and hard as he looked. Last night he hadn't even removed his shirt. His boxers hung low on his narrow hips and she could see the sexy V his hips made, pointing to the one place on him she'd never dared imagine on him.

"What?" he asked, and her eyes jumped back to his face.

"What? What?" she asked, then was shocked to realize the game they were playing, and it dawned on her what he'd probably been thinking about her. She blushed right down to her toes. He'd been looking at her earlier the way she was looking at him just now.

The room was quiet as they looked at each other. What could she say? Should she say anything? She was no good at sex games. She'd never... well ... never.

Then his phone rang, breaking the spell. He walked across the room, tossing the wet towel on the chair, something he knew drove Katie nuts. Before he could answer the phone, she was across the room, grabbing the towel before the water could soak into the chair's material, ruining it.

He watched her with a wicked smile, "Hello?"

She glared at him as she started to fold the wet towel, so she could hang it.

"What?" He almost dropped the phone. "No! She's here. No, I swear. Yeah, okay. No, I don't think that would be wise. Yeah, you do that. Bye."

"What?" she asked looking at his face.

"Well, it appears you've been kidnapped and a ransom of ten million dollars has been demanded from your family."

CHAPTER 6

"What!" she grabbed for his phone just as it rang again.

He handed it to her willingly, then walked over to where his food sat.

"Hello?"

"Katie! Thank God!" Her father's familiar voice sounded distant. Hearing him for the first time in over a year did something to her. She realized what kind of pain he must have gone through, what he must be going through now.

"Dad?" She walked to the window, trying to control her emotions. There was a buzzing in the background and she hoped the reception would be better by the window. "Dad, can you hear me?"

"Yes, honey. I'm so glad to hear that you're okay. We're on our way there. Our flight lands in less than two hours. Where are you?"

"We're just outside of Ioannina; we missed the flight to Italy." She didn't think that worrying her father with all the small details would gain her or him anything. She noticed that Jason's eyebrows shot up at her small omission.

"What's all this about me being kidnapped?"

"Probably just someone's sick joke. Ric and I will land soon. Honey get to Rome as quickly as you can, and please be careful." She heard her dad say something, most likely to her brother, then he was back, "Ric says to stay there, we're going to try to come to you."

"No, Dad," she said, knowing it wasn't safe where they were, that the men were looking for them. Jason had told her it was only another few hours to Igoumenitsa, and from there they could grab the ferry to Italy. They had plans to head out first thing in the morning. "We'll meet you in Rome in…"

She looked over at Jason, and he said, "Around three days, just to be safe."

"We'll meet you in Rome in three days. I'll give you a call then."

"Okay, just stay safe and try to stay in contact, okay?"

"Sure, Dad. Give Ric my love." She closed the phone and started pacing the floor.

Now she was feeling guilty. She hadn't even called her father once in the last year. She'd missed Christmas, his birthday, Father's Day, her birthday. What kind of daughter had she been over the last year?

She had called and left a message for her brother Ric once, just after she'd arrived in Europe. It was on the day he'd married Roberta Stanton. Roberta had been the police officer assigned to help her brother find out who had murdered his assistant and stolen a bunch of artwork from his art galleries. She felt bad that she hadn't attended their wedding, but she had known her mother would be there and she couldn't handle seeing her.

She had apologized in the message for not being there for them but explained how she'd needed more time to work things out. She loved her brother. Knowing he was the only one who would stand by her had made her want to distance herself from him even more. Finding out that he was her half-brother didn't change the way she felt about him.

She'd cried that night after leaving the message for him. She knew that her brother had found happiness with Roberta and was very happy for them both. But then the sadness had consumed her, and she found herself sinking into the darkness of her mind again. So, the next morning she'd moved on to a new destination on her trip. Exploring and meeting the locals was keeping her mind from her family troubles.

Jason watched her pace the floor from his chair, his dinner left untouched, and he could tell she was working herself into a mental state, blaming herself for everything, no doubt. The television was still on the international news channel, but the volume was off. He watched as a picture of Katie flashed across the screen, so he walked over and turned up the volume.

"…Katie Derby, daughter of socialite Kathleen Derby and oil tycoon Rodrick Derby the Third, and biological daughter of Damiano Cardone, head of Europe's mega business, New Edges. Miss Derby was last spotted in Alimos, just south of Athens, wearing a light green windbreaker and dark jeans, and carrying a black backpack. Miss Derby made headlines last year when it became known about her mother's…"

Katie walked up and flipped off the television, "I won't do this again."

She sat on the edge of the bed, chewing her bottom lip. He knew she only did that when she was really stressed out. Walking over to her, he nudged her so that her back faced him and he started rubbing the stress from her shoulders. He knew her weak spots, he knew her ticklish spots, he knew everything about her. After all, they'd been best friends forever and he knew every detail about her. Just as she knew everything about him.

Looking at the back of her head, he remembered a scene from a few years ago. They had just moved into the tiny two-bedroom place together, and he'd been dating Kimberly at the time. Katie had gone out a few times with his friend Tom, a relationship he didn't condone.

Tom was a lot like Jason, but Tom had a cocky attitude that Jason had never had. Tom thought he was good-looking, he thought that all the girls liked him, and it showed.

Jason only put up with his friend going out with Katie because he knew Katie didn't have much dating experience. He just wanted her to get out there, but after their fourth date, Jason sat her down and had the talk. He could tell that Tom was getting bored; he liked the faster girls. And Katie, well, he knew she was just tolerating him.

"Katie, Tom just isn't right for you." He sat across their small living room and gave her that look, the one that says, 'I'm trying to break it to you gently.'

"Oh, I know that." She'd tucked her feet up under her on the couch. They had just settled down after their double

dates and Kimberly was waiting for him in the next room. He didn't like her sleeping over, but she was determined, and he tolerated it.

"Jason, I'm not falling for him." She shrugged her shoulders. "I've just been having fun." She moved to turn on the television set, no doubt to sit back and watch an old TV show.

"Besides, I met this totally cute guy in my Physics class yesterday." Katie gave Jason a look of excitement.

He knew she was lying then; he could see it in her eyes. She had been having fun with Tom, but there had been something else she wasn't telling him, something he still didn't know about to this day. A few days after that, Tom broke it off with Katie and she had acted almost relieved. It had made him question whether there was someone else she was attracted to.

Looking at the back of her head, he could tell that was the case now, that she was keeping something from him. "Kat," he said to her back.

"Don't, I'm not in the mood to hear the speech right now." She rolled her shoulders, something she'd always done, but this time, he couldn't help focusing on how soft her skin looked on her neck.

He could feel the tension radiating from her. Knowing a simple back rub wouldn't take her mind off her family, he dipped his head and ran his lips along her soft skin. She froze. He pushed her hair to the side as he continued to run his mouth up and down her delicate neck, tasting her, enjoying the feel of her vibrating in his hands.

"Jason?" it was a whisper.

"Just relax, you smell and taste so good."

"Oh, my…"

He ran his hands down her arms, then when he'd enjoyed every inch of her neck, she turned to face him, and she just looked at him.

Her hands came up to his hair and pulled him down to her mouth. He could feel her fingers flex and relax while holding him close.

"God, Katie." He ran his hands downwards and then started back up under her light shirt, playing with the soft skin just underneath as she ran her hands over him lightly.

He pulled her closer, so he could feel her every breath, and to his delight, she rolled her head back, exposing her long neck.

He felt her breathing as his fingers lightly played over her ribs, upward, until finally, he cupped her and moaned at the sheer pleasure he found. Toying with the tight bud, he circled it slowly until she moaned in return. Taking his time, he slowly reached over and did the same to her other nipple. Then he bent his head and lifted her shirt as he ran his tongue slowly over her, following the same pattern.

She leaned farther back, her hands behind her, supporting her weight. Jason rolled them onto the bed without removing his mouth from her heated skin. Now she was sprawled out for his pleasure. He'd quickly removed her shirt and tossed it on the floor. Looking down at her, he watched as her eyes fluttered open.

"Jason?"

"Shh, you're beautiful. So beautiful. I'd never imagined." He dipped his head and licked his way around her soft skin. Her hands went back to his hair, holding him to her as she moaned in pleasure. She was very vocal, and he was enjoying hearing the sexy little sounds emanating from her. Running his hands slowly up and down her soft legs, he pushed them open a little wider as his fingers brushed over the tender spot just below her soft cotton shorts. He felt her tense and slowly moved his hand away until he felt her relax again.

Then he ran his fingers under the top of the shorts, pulling them down as he kissed the newly exposed skin. Looking up to gauge her reaction, he saw her eyes, watching him. The dimples on either side of her smile flashed and he saw her dark eyes close slowly on a moan. Taking the hint, he pulled her shorts down, exposing her to his view for the first time in the full light.

"Beautiful." He kissed her flat stomach, running his fingers across her belly until he finally cupped her softly. Her back arched off the bed and her hands gripped his head as he bent to taste her just there.

He slid one finger in, enjoying the gasps and moans as she moved her hips to the motion. He found the noises she was making totally exotic. He knew she was tight, so he stretched her, placing two fingers inside her slick heat, slowly circling and toying until he could tell she was building and ready to explode. Looking up, he watched her and knew he'd never forget the look of Katie during a peak.

Katie watched as he relaxed beside her and knew she had no plans for tonight to follow the same pattern as last night. Rolling onto her side, she slid her leg over his, running her hands over his bare chest. She watched as his eyes heated.

"Katie?"

"Shhh." She put her fingers over his mouth, then ran her lips and tongue over his chest, enjoying rolling her tongue over his flat nipples until they peaked, much like hers had. She nibbled on them with her teeth and his hands went into her hair, trying to hold her still. She moved lower down his stomach, enjoying the play of muscles that ran down across each rib and over his muscular stomach. She loved his sexy six pack and couldn't stop playing her fingers over the dips.

When she came across a new scar on his left rib, she looked up at him.

"Where did you get this?" She traced the line with her finger.

"Hmm, I got nipped by a bull when you decided you wanted to take part in the running of the bulls in Spain."

"You were there for the festival?" She smiled, remembering the thrill she'd had climbing the fence, getting away from the bulls, not to mention the week-long party she'd enjoyed. Oh, she'd never been in any real danger, but watching the bulls and people run by had been a thrill.

"Yes, I got caught in the crowd and ended up in front of a very big, brown bull." He ran his hands through her hair.

She traced the line of his scar, happy to know that he'd somehow been a part of her reckless behavior. Then she ran her tongue over the line and he moaned, and she moved lower, past his belly button. He held onto her head until she used her teeth to pull his boxers down his narrow hips, then he fisted his hands beside him on the bed. She looked at him and noticed he was watching her with his clouded, dark blue eyes.

Using her hands, she pushed his shorts lower over his

sexy hips until finally, she saw all of him. He was bigger than she imagined, and she was starting to have second thoughts. But she never backed away from a challenge, and she saw him as just that.

Running her hand over the length of him, she noticed that he was holding his breath and watching her very closely. She ran her fingers up and down him lightly, and he almost jumped in her hands.

Smiling, she leaned over and placed a soft kiss on the head, then using her tongue, she rolled her mouth around the tip until she felt him go stiff. She licked the entire length from bottom to top and then took him into her mouth, deep into her throat, until she felt his hands in her hair again. He tasted sexy and she couldn't get enough of enjoying him.

Rolling her tongue around as she took him deep, she enjoyed the feel and taste of him as she pleased him. He moaned her name and she heard him begging her.

"My God, Katie, I'm going to come in your mouth if you keep that up." His hands were in her hair.

She looked up into his eyes, "You promise?" Then she went back to torturing him until she felt his hot seed flood her mouth, and the tangy taste of him almost undid her. She lightly licked every inch of him clean.

Then she moved up the bed and whispered, "Now we're even."

He chuckled. "No, not even close," he said, and he pulled her to him.

"Jason?"

"Shh, Katie, I know what you want. Just let me hold

you now." He put his face into her hair and she could have sworn he started snoring.

It had always been this way with him. Not them laying naked together, but he'd always been able to fall asleep quickly.

When they had been living together, on nights when they were both free they'd end up watching old TV shows or movies in the living room. She would always hear him snoring in the chair if he was too tired to enjoy a full movie. She chuckled at the almost child-like ability he had at shutting himself down, and kind of envied it.

Laying there in the dark, her mind kept running over and over how she was going to finally get what she wanted from him. By the time her eyes closed, she thought she had her plan all laid out.

Katie woke the next morning and blinked a few times before she realized she was in the bed alone. Stretching her hands over her head, she smiled to herself, remembering the night before. She'd never thought something like that was possible, let alone that it would feel so... so... awesome!

Looking around the room, she wondered where he was. Quickly getting up, she went to clean up in the bathroom. As she reached for the door handle, she heard him talking on the other side of the door. She leaned her head against the door, silently wishing for a glass to hold up against the wood so she could hear better.

"No, I told you, I didn't speak to anyone. It's like they were waiting for us. – Yeah, I know. – Okay, are you sure? – You know she's not going to like – yeah – okay."

She quickly jumped back in the bed when she heard him walking towards the door. Shutting her eyes quickly, she tried to slow her breathing.

The door opened, and she wished she'd had the forethought to turn her head away from the bathroom.

"You're not fooling me, you know."

She sat up and smiled at him. "I don't know what you mean." Getting up quickly, she tried to walk around him to get into the bathroom.

He blocked her easily with his arm. "Katie, we have to maintain phone silence until we get to Rome to meet your dad and brother."

She looked at him and noticed that he had shaved that morning. She wanted to run her hands over the smooth surface, but instead, she asked, "Why?"

"Just a hunch," he said and when she continued to stare at him, he took a deep breath, "Okay, I think they knew we were heading to the airport. They were waiting there, not at the bus station, not the train station. The airport. Doesn't that seem a little odd?"

She thought about it, and now that he mentioned it, it was weird. "Well, maybe there were others waiting at the other places."

"No, I don't think so. I think someone told them where we were headed and how we were traveling to get there. I think they will be watching all the routes to Rome."

"Well, then," tossing up her hands she started pacing the floor, "what are we going to do? Not go?"

"No, we're just going to have to take less traveled routes."

"What did you have in mind?"

He walked to her and placed a light kiss on her forehead.

"We'd better be going."

"Jason, I hate it when you leave me in the dark. I'm not going anywhere until I know exactly what it is you have planned." She crossed her arms and glared at him.

Four hours later they were sitting on a bus driving south and Katie felt defeated. How did he have such power over her? She glared at him as he sat in the seat across from hers.

"I hate you, you know."

"That's nice," he said, not looking up from the news-paper he was pretending to read. She knew he wasn't really reading it because it was all in Greek.

"You can't even read that." She pushed it down until he was looking at her. "You promised me some answers. Since we're stuck on this bus for over an hour, now is the perfect time for you to give me some."

He leaned closer to her and she could smell his musky scent and wanted to lean into him but held back and kept her arms crossed. She hoped that she had a determined look on her face, fooling him into giving her those answers.

"Fine," he leaned back. "I was hired to track you down by your family. I've been following you since September. There, are you happy?" He lifted the paper again, so she grabbed it, wadded it up, and tossed it on the floor.

"I know all that, the question I want to be answered is... Who?"

"Who, what?"

"We are not playing this game. Who hired you?"

"Does it really matter?"

"Yes! If it was her, I'm getting off this bus right now and you can kiss my…"

"Really?" Instead of looking shocked, he had the most devilish grin on his face. Then she realized what she had been about to say and what he had done to her last night, and her face turned beet red.

It took her almost a full minute for the heat in her body to dissipate.

"Jason, tell me who hired you."

"No."

"Then you've just confirmed that it was her." She moved to stand up, and he grabbed her by the arm and pushed her into the seat next to his.

"Stop this, you're not going anywhere. Why does it matter who's been fronting my bills? What matters is, I've been following you to make sure you're okay."

"Fronting your bills? We both know why she hired you. Why she picked you for the job is a mystery to me, but this is just her way of keeping me under her wing. Her vicious, cheating, controlling wing. I don't care what she has paid you, the fact that you have even been talking to her makes you a traitor in my book." She was working herself into an emotional state. She was upset that she'd let it go this long. This time when she got up to move, he grabbed his bag and followed her. When she finally convinced the driver to stop, Jason followed her off the bus.

"No! You don't get to get off the bus now!" She tried to push him back on, but he just laughed at her until she turned and stormed off down the road.

Now she was still stuck with him, the biggest traitor

imaginable, and they were in the middle of... looking around, Katie realized there was nothing but hills and grass. Nowhere, again! She could just make out the bus as it disappeared over a hill.

"Augh!" She tossed down her bag and rounded on him. "You! How could you do this? First, you embarrass me at the party, then at the coffee shop, then on national television. And now ..." She poked him in the chest, but he didn't even blink. She turned and started pacing; she was on a roll and didn't want to stop. "Now you're taking her money, sleeping with the enemy so-to-speak, doing her bidding, stabbing me in the back, selling me down the river, no... worse," she pointed her finger in his face, "Judas..." she was almost running out of steam, so she turned and started pacing again.

"Are you almost done?" he asked with a tight smile.

"No!" she rounded on him again. The hurt showed on her face and she knew the moment he saw it. "Why her? Why not my brother or my fathers, either one of them?"

He walked forward and took her shoulders in his hands gently. "Katie, she was the only one who asked me. She was frantic those first weeks. She called me almost daily, asking if I knew anything about where you would have gone. Then a few months after your parents' divorce was final, she asked me to follow your trail and she paid my way. She just wanted to know that you were okay."

He pulled her close and just held on. "To be honest, I was just about to come after you myself if she hadn't asked me. I would have done it for free, but she insisted on paying for the travel expenses. You really scared everyone, leaving the way you did, not taking a phone, not contacting anyone to let us know where you were or that you were okay."

"I know, I just needed this time. I needed to experience life outside of being Katie Derby, daughter of two high-powered men. Being stuck between two major corporations on opposite sides of the globe with the media in your face does something to you." How had he turned this around on her? He always had a way of diffusing the situation.

"I'm sorry, I can't imagine it. I know how it felt seeing our friends betray our trust."

She looked at him and realized he had lost everyone back home, too, that she wasn't the only one who'd been put under the media microscope. She remembered some of the interviews by their friends. Everyone had highlighted their relationship, trying to make it something that it hadn't been.

"Come on, we'd better start walking if we plan on getting anywhere." He pulled back and smiled at her.

"I'm sorry." She took her bag after he handed it to her. "I just couldn't spend any more time on that bus. I'm sure there's another bus stop around, and a little walking hasn't hurt us so far." She tried to smile away her frustration and the possibility of her feet hurting again that night. "Besides, it couldn't be as bad as the other day."

Less than an hour later the rain started, and she felt totally hopeless.

"Don't say anything." She looked over at him as the heavy rain soaked them both.

So far there hadn't been any towns. They'd passed a few quiet farmhouses and had seen plenty of cows, sheep, and horses. There hadn't even been other cars or vehicles on the road. They really were in the middle of nowhere.

He grabbed her hand and they sprinted to an old building that they had spotted in an open field. It was an old gray barn which looked like it had seen better days. It appeared that no one had used it in years.

Katie watched as Jason broke the old lock that kept the door closed. It was rusted all the way through and when he opened the small door, it almost came off its hinges. The place smelled like mold and dust, but it was dry and a little warmer. At least it was out of the cool wind that was now blowing across the fields.

Dropping her bag inside the door, she searched inside it for her flashlight, only to realize it had been stolen. A light filled the room and she turned to see Jason with his flashlight.

Searching the room, they found some bales of old hay and a large tractor that looked like it hadn't been used since the early fifties.

"Well, at least we won't sleep on flour bags tonight," he said, walking over to the hay. He pulled out a pocket knife and cut the ropes that had been holding the hay together. Then he took his time making a large pallet out of the fresher hay from inside the bales. He took the large black blanket that had covered the back seat of the tractor, shook it off, then laid it over the hay. Once he was done, he moved his bag over and pulled out a small brown bag and a large bottle of water.

"Where did you get those?" She looked over at with excitement.

CHAPTER 7

"*Y*ou didn't think I would come unprepared, did you?" He chuckled at the face she made.

She sat down on the blanket in the hay next to him and removed her wet jacket. He discovered her light cotton shirt underneath was completely soaked and see-through but decided against telling her he could see every inch of her. It took all his willpower to hand her a sandwich and the water without his eyes popping out of their sockets.

Did she know what she did to him? She sat there completely focused on the food. He realized he was hungry, too, but it wasn't the sandwich he wanted.

He had missed his friendship with her over the last year. But in the last few days, that friendship had grown into something he hadn't realized was there before. He'd tried to deny his attraction to her and for the most part, he'd kept it at bay. But now, even watching her eat food looked appealing. How had she changed so much that she could seduce his thoughts with a simple sandwich and a bottle of water?

He thought about what he'd done to her last night, what she'd done to him. He was getting hard thinking about her mouth on his skin. He wanted her naked underneath him, to feel her skin against his own skin. To have his hands on her, his fingers inside her heat. For him to be inside her heat.

He watched as she leaned her head back and took a long drink of the cool water. He had to swallow the desire in his throat. His eyes roamed down her body again. Her nipples peeked out from her wet shirt and he wondered if she was wearing a bra because he could see everything. He thought he could just bend his head slightly and in one move have her nipple in his mouth, sucking.

Shaking his head clear, he said, "Katie?" and when she looked over at him, her eyes showed him that she knew exactly what she'd been doing to him. He tried to smile, but then she licked her bottom lip slowly, to remove a small breadcrumb from the corner. The small dimples that played at the corner of her sweet, soft looking mouth flashed and he didn't even remember pulling her into his lap.

The kiss was hotter than any he'd ever had; it warmed his cool skin, causing a light steam to rise from him. He had toyed with her for two days, building his desires, gauging her reaction and not once did he think that he was torturing himself in the process.

She didn't fight the kiss but tried to pull him closer, so he pulled her to him, devouring her, tasting her. With shaky hands he started undoing the small buttons that ran down the front of her shirt, slowly peeling the wet material aside so he could see her, just her.

She shivered when he finally had her exposed to his view. She started to pull his jacket off his shoulders, so he helped her and flung the wet coat on top of his bag.

Then she was reaching for his shirt and he helped her remove it as well. Small bumps covered them both from the chill in the air. Slowly, he laid her back until his body covered hers.

Running kisses down her neck, he enjoyed the sounds she made as she ran her hands up and down his arms. He could tell how shy she was with her touch and he wanted to reassure her.

"You can touch me, Katie. I want to feel your hands on me, everywhere."

He felt her pull back but couldn't really see her in the darkened room. He wished for more light, but he didn't dare leave the flashlight on all day. The light that was coming from under the door would have to be sufficient, since the clouds were blocking out the sun, and the dreariness would most likely continue through the night.

As she looked into her eyes, her hands started moving to his stomach, his back, his hips. It was pure torture feeling her cool, soft fingers run over him lightly.

"I want your hands on me, too. I love how you make me feel."

He followed her lead and ran his hands to where her wet jeans hindered his downward path. Slowly, with his eyes on her, he unbuttoned them and took the zipper in his fingers.

"Are you sure?"

When she nodded her head, he pulled his mouth back

down to hers and knew he didn't ever want to stop. Couldn't stop. She tasted like spring. Their skin was slowly drying but he could taste the fresh raindrops on her and enjoyed lapping them up. He could feel her vibrate under his touch.

Pulling wet jeans down her slender body was harder work then he imagined. He thought there was probably a bead of sweat on his brow when he finally freed her legs for his view. She had wiggled and laughed when he'd cursed the wet denim. He got his jeans off in half the time and knelt over her with just his damp boxers on.

Now she was lying there, the white of her wet panties a beacon in the darkness. Her skin was darker than his, and her dark eyes and hair made her look like a Greek goddess laid out for his pleasure.

Her mouth pouted slightly until he ran his hands up her legs. He watched her eyes closed and her head tilted back while he touched her. Then he held up her leg and ran his tongue up it and she moaned as she grabbed his hair. He ran his mouth up her as he pulled the small cotton over her hips and down her long legs. Then his fingers found her heat, wet and slick, waiting for him.

"God, Katie, I don't, I can't…" his ability to think had disappeared.

Her hands were on his stomach and he felt her tugging at his boxers, then he was freed, and he kicked them down near his feet. He kissed her, feeling her relax totally under his hands as his fingers went back to her heat and played there. He parted her soft lips slowly and enjoyed the slickness he found. Running his finger across her, he watched her hips rise and fall and heard her moaning his name as he circled her wet heat with his finger. Then he pushed a finger into her and her shoulders came off the blanket. He had to have her now. He reached for his backpack and accidentally grabbed hers instead.

"What?" She watched him hunting for his bag.

"What?" He looked back over at her. "I'm looking for my backpack."

"Why?" She started to sit up and crossed her arms over her beautiful chest.

"I have a…" he found it then and held up the small foil packages.

"Ohhh," He could instantly tell she was uncomfortable and he rushed back over to her, trying not to chuckle.

"I told you I was prepared." Then he kissed away her discomfort until he finally felt her relax again in his arms. He pushed her legs wider with his hands and ran his finger up and down her entrance until she moved her hips, matching what he was doing to her.

Then he moved over her and kissed her until he was blind with lust. Slowly he started to enter her and when he found himself blocked, he stopped and looked down at her.

"Katie?"

"Don't stop now Jason, my God, don't you dare stop." She was holding very still, and her nails were digging into his shoulders. Her legs had wrapped around his hips trying to hold him closer.

In one quick motion, he took her as she screamed.

"I'm sorry, baby," he whispered into her hair. If she wanted him to stop now, there was no way he could. Then he started to move slowly, and he could tell she was enjoying herself. Her fingers dug into his hips and shoulders, and she was raising her hips to match his thrusts.

"Katie, wait, just … let's slow down." He needed a

107

minute, he didn't think he could wait for her, but she just held on and kept moving her hips under him.

When she screamed his name, he was two seconds behind her.

It must have been the owl that woke her. At first, she didn't know what the noise was, then she recognized a distinct "hoot" and relaxed into the warmth of Jason's chest.

"Are you okay?" he asked. She felt the rumble of his voice and laughed at how different it sounded with her ear to his chest.

"Yes, I'm wonderful," she said, as he sat up and started hunting in his bag again.

"What are you looking for now?" She sat up and tried to see what he was doing, but it was too dark in the barn and all she could do was listen to the rain outside and him moving around.

Then a beam of light hit her square in the eyes.

"Oops, sorry." He dropped the light to her chest and she quickly covered herself with her hands as he laughed. "Sorry, again," he said, but he didn't move the light away from her body and she closed her eyes on a wave of embarrassment. She wished for the dark again.

"My God, Katie, you're beautiful." She heard him moving closer and kept her eyes closed as she pulled her legs up to her chest.

"Here," he said, and then he was quiet, so she opened her eyes and saw that he had a small bag of baby wipes that he was trying to hand her. "I thought you might want to clean up a bit. I'm starving so I'm going to eat my sandwich. You can use the light if you need to…"

She looked down and noticed that she did need to clean herself. Taking the wipes and the light from him, she waited until he turned his back on her before she started cleaning.

"Why didn't you tell me that you'd never had sex before?"

She shook her head and was very glad he was looking away from her, so he couldn't see her beet red face. "I guess the subject never came up."

"If I had known you hadn't done that before, I could have…"

"Stop, don't you dare say you would have changed anything. It was perfect."

She heard him chuckle as she grabbed a dry shirt from her bag and her extra pair of jeans, then slipped them on. The barn was cool, and she felt herself shivering. She took their wet clothes and hung them over the bucket of the tractor, so they could dry in the cool, night air. When she turned back around, he was watching her with a smile on his face.

"What?"

"Did I ever tell you that I like it that you're so crazy about cleaning up after me?"

"Many times. You know my brother always wonders how I can be so messy when I visit him and be so clean the rest of the time." She walked over and sat next to him. "I tell him it's because when I visit him, it's like a vacation from my A-type personality."

He chuckled at her and she loved the sound he made.

She'd always liked his laugh. Even when they had been younger, she'd found it intriguing and outright sexy.

"I think you leave your stuff lying around just so I can clean it up." She tried to reach for his sandwich and he held it out of her reach.

She crossed her arms and tried for her best pouting face.

"Fine, you can have the rest of my sandwich if I get dessert."

"You have dessert in that bag?" she asked hopefully.

When he just smiled at her, his meaning dawned on her and she felt the heat spreading throughout her body. Slowly, keeping her eyes on him, she reached over and took the last bite he held out. She watched his eyes, and they were glued to her mouth as she nibbled on the last little piece of the sourdough bread. When she licked her lips, his eyes followed the movement of her tongue, and she actually thought she saw him quiver.

Did she really have this much power over him? He was just staring at her mouth like he wanted to devour her. She moved slowly and brushed her lips against his and watched his eyes as she flipped off the flashlight, sending them into darkness.

She thought the darkness would help quench her thirst for him, but instead, her desire increased since now she could feel and hear everything.

She felt his fingers brush against her neck as he plunged his hands into her hair, holding her mouth to his own hot kisses. She smelled his aftershave and cologne, a sexy mix with the hay and cool night air. She heard him moan when she flicked her tongue across his and felt him catch his breath when she reached down and found him hard and naked.

As she took his length into her hands, she felt shy, like she'd do something wrong any minute. But when he just sat there, unmoving, she continued to lightly trace his length with her fingers. Then she gripped him lightly and heard him moan with delight. His hands tightened in her hair slightly, and she could tell he'd forgotten that he still had a hold of her. His length was warm and hard in her hand; she enjoyed the soft skin and marveled at the contrast.

She moved closer and kissed him on the neck, just below his ear and jaw, and felt his beard from the day's growth scratch her chin lightly. He tasted musky and sexy, and she wanted to lick him all over. She ran her mouth and tongue down his neck and could feel his muscles tense as she passed his shoulders. She moved her mouth down his chest as she kept lightly stroking him, not sure if what she was doing was giving him as much pleasure as he'd given her. When she reached his flat nipple, she traced it with her tongue and heard him whisper her name.

"What?" she asked against his heated flesh. "What do you want, Jason?"

"You, just you, Katie." He brought her mouth back to his and leaned back until she lay across his chest. "I don't want to hurt you; I think there is some rule about waiting a while after your first time."

"You know that I don't always follow rules."

He kissed her again and said against her lips, "The condoms are right there, do you think you can…?" he left the question open.

She felt around and found the small package. Opening

it with her teeth, she felt the small disk in her hands and ran her fingers over the slick softness. Which way did it go on? What if she broke it trying to put it on him? Worse, what if she hurt him trying to get it on?

"Stop overthinking things, just slide it on," he chuckled.

Taking her time, she grabbed him in one hand and slowly rolled the condom on, enjoying the feeling of the new texture over him.

"Now, sit up and slide on."

What did he mean by that?

"Up on your knees. Come on, Kat, you're killing me here," he moaned.

She moved until she sat above him, straddling him with her knees on either side of his hips. With one hand flat on his chest, she held herself up as the other hand gripped him and positioned him outside her opening. Then she slowly slid down, impaling herself fully as she moaned with delight.

"Oh, I like this," she said into the dark.

She heard him chuckle. "So, do I. Now ride me, Katie."

She started moving her hips slowly and then his hands grasped her, helping her find the rhythm until they were both breathless and sweaty.

She moved her legs up, so she could squat over him and move up and down on him, and she felt him start to stiffen.

"Oh my God!" he said, and she noticed he was holding very still.

"What, Jason?" She smiled into the darkness.

"You feel so good. Kat, I want…" He reached up and

placed a finger just outside her entrance, then he lightly touched her, and she exploded around him.

She tried to slide down and lay across his chest, but he reversed their positions quickly. He grabbed one of her legs and held it close to her chest as he moved more quickly above her. His hips were thrusting harder and faster than she could bear.

"Come again for me, Kat." He moved faster and lengthened his thrusts until she felt her building again.

"Jason," she wanted to know that he was with her this time, "please." She threw her head back and closed her eyes on a wave of pure pleasure.

He went still just as she screamed his name.

He lay there for a few minutes listening to her heartbeat slow down. She'd destroyed him. He could feel her skin cooling and knew when she'd fallen asleep. She snuggled closer and he could feel the evening chill. He pulled out his zip-up sweatshirt and draped it over her shoulders. Trying to snuggle closer for body warmth, she mumbled into his chest.

He loved the feel of her in his arms, naked. The last two evenings he'd enjoyed sleeping with her. He realized that he'd never really allowed anyone to sleep over, except Kimberly. She'd insisted, and he hadn't wanted the sex to go away, so he'd caved. There were some people you just couldn't stand to snuggle with after sex, and Kimberly had been one of those people. She'd hogged the bed, her feet were always icy, and she snored, loudly. It had been one of the reason's he'd finally broken it off with her. Actually, the main reason was that she and Katie didn't get along. Oh, he knew the games Kimberly had been playing, trying to get him to choose her over Katie, something he would never have done.

But the last straw had been when she started talking about moving into the apartment after Katie moved back to the dorms. She had even hinted at marriage. He shivered now thinking about his life with Kimberly.

Then he thought of how it would be to be married to Katie and an inner peace fell over his mind and his heart.

When had he fallen in love with her? He couldn't pinpoint the exact moment. Maybe it was that first day by the pool? Maybe when he'd accidentally brushed up against her boobs in junior high and gotten his first boner? Maybe it was two days ago when he'd rescued her on the beach and she'd knocked some sense into him, and his jaw?

Brushing his hand over her hair, he listened to her breathing and knew that he'd always been in love with her. It had just been hidden. Kissing her hair, he smiled into the darkness and knew he had to make things right between them. He knew he was keeping secrets from her about her family and he didn't want to keep anything from her. First thing in the morning, he would come clean.

He closed his eyes and listened to her heartbeat with his own and dreamed of the day they had met.

CHAPTER 8

hen Jason woke up the next morning, the first thing he saw was an owl's butt hovering over his face. Quickly moving his head, he looked up at the truss and at the owl and laughed as he sat up.

"What?" Katie woke with a start and jumped up from beside him. The morning sun was up and the dark barn had enough light that he could see her standing next to him totally naked, which made him forget what he was laughing about.

"What! What is it? Is it a snake?" She looked around in the hay, afraid, standing up on her tiptoes. He laughed again as she glared at him. "There are a lot of snakes around here. I had one fall on my head once while I was walking under a tree. Have I ever told you that I can't stand snakes?"

"No," he laughed again as she tried to climb on the tractor, butt naked. "It's just an owl." He pointed to the large brown bird as it sat on a wood rafter right above where they'd been lying.

She stopped and looked at him, then looked up at the owl. "You have me jumping around naked over a stupid owl?" She walked over and grabbed her shirt and jeans. He enjoyed seeing her backside as she pulled on her jeans, sans underwear. Then she put on her shirt without a bra and he lost all ability to think when she turned around. He could see everything under the light t-shirt.

"You are not going out like that," he said as he stalked closer to her.

"Like what?" She was trying to put on her shoes, but she had sat down to dust off the bottom of her feet first.

He walked over and yanked her bra and panties off the bucket of the tractor. "Here, put these on."

She looked at them, then at him, and laughed. "Really, Jason. I'm just going to step outside to go to the bathroom and freshen up. Who do you think is going to be out there to see me dressed like this?"

"I don't care," he growled. She just looked at him as he stood there, holding out her undergarments. Finally, she reached up and grabbed them from him.

"Fine." She pulled her shirt back off quickly. "But I'm only putting on the bra for now." She quickly dressed again and grabbed the baby wipes, then walked towards the front door of the barn.

She picked up her bag and left just as the owl let out a loud "hoot", which almost sounded like a laugh, to him.

"Shut up, no one asked you," he mumbled to the bird and then turned to get dressed himself.

❄

Katie stood outside and hugged herself, then spun in a quick circle. She'd never imagined that love would feel this good, that sex with him would feel this good. She felt alive, and for the first time in over a year, she was happy. Truly happy.

Looking around, she saw that the sun was already up, warming the dew on the grass and causing the mist to hover over the green fields. The clean air hit her full force and she took a large breath, enjoying the fresh smells. There were hills covered with wildflowers on either side of the old barn and she watched as a bus and several cars sped past on the road a few yards away. Knowing they had a full day of walking ahead of them, she walked around to the back of the barn to relieve herself.

She used the wipes to clean her hands and face and was almost feeling human again, ten minutes later. She was even lucky enough to find a mint at the bottom of her bag and sucked on it to freshen her breath.

When she turned to go back inside the barn, she ran into a large chest.

"Well, well, what have we here?" The English was so heavily accented; she could hardly make out what the man was saying. Katie recognized him immediately and screamed for Jason, then she tried to kick out and bite the man's hand as he slapped something over her mouth. She tried to fight him off, kicking and pushing his hands away, but then she was plunged into darkness.

Jason woke several hours later in the back of a vehicle. His head was killing him, and he could feel dried blood over the largest bump he'd ever received. When he opened his eyes, he actually saw double. He'd heard that expression before, but to experience it first hand was something indescribable. His stomach rolled, and he tried breathing through the pain.

The last thing he remembered was bending down to put on his shoes. Had he gotten them on? He wiggled his feet and realized he was indeed wearing both shoes. Then his mind cleared. Katie!

Looking around, he cursed the double vision; his eyes wouldn't focus on anything. He could tell they were still moving since he felt the familiar rumble and motions of being in a vehicle. Since he was able to stretch out his full six-foot-one frame, he knew he wasn't in the trunk of a car, so he gathered he had to be in a van or a truck of some kind. Trying to move his hands, he realized they were tied behind his back. Rolling over, he felt a soft body next to his and realized Katie was there. She must be knocked out since she hadn't moved when he'd touched her. He saw red as he thought about the men hitting her over the head like they had hit him. She could be bleeding, or worse.

"Oh, looks like this one is awake. You must not have hit him as hard as you think." The accent was thick, and the English was very bad. But Jason instantly knew who was speaking due to the slight nasal sounds. Broken nose guy and his minions had found them.

"What did you do to Katie? Where are you taking us?"

"Oh, he thinks he gets answers." He heard two men chuckle. Where were the others?

"What did you do to Katie?" he said more forcefully.

"Miss Derby is not hurt like you; we use sleeping

powder. She's to be delivered untouched. You on the other foot, not so much."

"Other hand, Mikolas," his colleague jumped in.

"Oh?"

"It's on the other hand, I think."

"Oh, yes, Raul, you are right. You, on the other hand, not so much." They both chuckled.

Jason's mind was too foggy to register their conversation, but his fingers had found his pocket knife. The thugs had forgotten to frisk him. Slowly removing it, he pulled it open and started working on the ropes behind his back.

"Where are you taking us?" He knew he needed to keep them talking or distracted so they couldn't hear what he was doing. Even if he couldn't completely focus on their faces, he could tell that broken nose guy no longer looked over his shoulder at him.

"We are going to get paid." They both laughed. "We are getting paid big for that little one. For you, I think maybe we just feed to the sharks." They both laughed and started speaking in Greek, or what Jason assumed was Greek. He recognized a few words, but they were talking too fast for him to catch anything important.

Jason finally got his hands free and twisted so he could start working on releasing his legs.

He listened to them speaking and thought he heard them say "Derby", "millions", and "ferry".

When his feet were finally freed, he moved over and felt for Katie. Realizing that they hadn't even tied her hands or feet, he lay there and tried to think of his next move.

How was he supposed to fight these two off if he couldn't even see straight? Plus, the vehicle was moving too fast for him to make a jump for it. If he tried something while they were still moving, well, he didn't think his head could stand a car accident. So, he stayed still and kept trying to focus his eyes.

Less than an hour later, he could feel the turns and stops of being back in a large town or city. He reached over and tried to see if Katie was awake, but she didn't move. He would just have to carry her after he took care of these two. Somehow.

When they came to a stop, he watched as the bigger man, Mikolas, got out while the smaller man, Raul, sat behind the wheel, looking off in the distance.

Moving slowly, he got up onto the balls of his feet and looked out. He could see Mikolas out in front of the van, talking to a large man. The pair stood by a small boat and he could tell they were at a small marina.

Moving quickly, he put his sharp pocket knife against the other man's throat.

"Don't move." When the man nodded, he asked, "Where are we?" Jason watched the two men on the dock. They were in a heated discussion and he watched as the larger man reached for his wallet.

"Igoumenitsa docks."

"Where are the other men that were looking for us?"

"What other men?"

"Don't mess around with me. The other men at the airport."

"They went ahead to Rome. They will be watching the airport and bus stations for you."

"Who wants Katie?" He watched as the men argued some more and knew that his time was running out.

"I don't know. Mikolas deals with that."

He bent down and grabbed the tire iron he'd seen earlier, probably the one they'd used on his head, then he hit the man, knocking him out.

He quickly stepped over Katie, then quietly opened the back doors. Picking Katie up, he tossed her lightly over his shoulders. She didn't move. When he sprinted for the first building, which was just a few feet away, he realized how dizzy he was. He didn't hear any shouting and hoped he'd gotten away, unnoticed. When he reached the corner, he ducked behind it and continued to run until they were a dozen blocks away. He weaved through the empty side streets, taking different routes so they didn't travel in a straight line. He felt a little drunk and was sure he looked that way, but it was almost impossible for him to walk in a straight line. Several times he'd ended up grabbing onto a wall of a building to steady himself.

Finally, when he hit a few larger streets, he started to pass people, and he was thankful no one said anything to him. Instead, they just looked at him funny, so he tried to avoid as many people as he could, keeping instead to back streets.

His vision was going gray around the edges and he was finding it harder to carry Katie. His breath was coming in quick bursts and he worried what would happen to them if he passed out. He tried hard to stay focused.

He didn't know where he was going but knew that they had to get as far away from the docks as possible until he could see straight. Several times he stumbled and almost fell, so he'd grabbed on to the wall and had been walking with his hand against it. He finally felt his energy wavering when he heard an angel.

"Parakalo?" A woman stepped in front of him, causing

him to come to a complete stop. She held her hands up and continued to speak to him in Greek.

"English?" he asked. He tried to hold onto her voice, tried to keep from passing out.

"Vai, yes, of course, do you need hospital? Is woman hurt?" He noticed then, that the young woman was wearing a nurse's outfit.

"Yes, she was given sleeping powder of some kind."

"Vai, parakalo. Yes, please, come with me to nosokomeio."

Jason looked at her not knowing what she was saying.

"Hospital."

He nodded slightly and followed the woman back about half a block to where he'd passed an older white building. Not seeing clearly, he'd run right by the hospital.

"Ohi, you are bleeding." She pointed to his head as they walked in the doors.

"Yes, I was hit and knocked out."

"Did you?" she made a motion like she was sleeping.

"Yes, I blacked out."

"Ohi kalo,"

Jason walked over and laid Katie down on a gurney the woman was motioning toward. When the woman gestured for him to lay down on the other one, he sat down facing Katie. He watched as an older doctor rushed in and started examining Katie.

"My name is Airlea, you?"

"Jason, and that's Katie."

"Kalós, you wait, I get better English."

Jason watched as the pretty brunette walked away, then he turned his attention to the doctor and nurse taking Katie's vitals.

Less than a minute later, a young boy around twelve walked back in the room with Airlea.

"This is Michael; he is English better."

"Hi, Michael." Jason looked down at a dark-haired boy. His clothes were bigger than they should have been and his hair was long and wavy. He wore a large smile on his face, but Jason could see concern in the young boy's eyes.

"Hello, Airlea wants to know what happened, was there an accident?"

"No, we were jumped." When the young boy just looked at him, he clarified. "Two men hit me and gave Katie some sleeping powder, or so they called it, then they put us in a van and brought us here. I knocked one over the head and we ran away until I ran into Airlea here."

The boy turned and translated.

"Ohi, Ohi kalo,"

"That's not good," Michael translated. Then the boy listened as Airlea asked more questions and turned to translate again.

"Airlea needs to know how long you blacked out for."

Katie could hear talking but couldn't understand any of it. Then something that smelled terrible was put in front of her face, and when she moved to push it away, a hand grabbed hers, holding it down until she coughed and opened her eyes.

"Vai, parakalo," a skinny, older man said, hovering over her. "Ágrypnos."

"Katie?" She heard Jason's voice and turned her head

towards him. He was sitting on a bed next to hers, with a young dark-haired boy standing close to him, and a beautiful, busty, brunette hovering over him. The woman's hand was on his knee, and Katie watched as she leaned closer to him, keeping her eyes on his face.

The woman was beautiful by any standard. Her dark skin glowed with rich, caramel colors and her eyes were big, dark, and beautiful. She had a figure that any woman would be jealous of. Her full, red lips made Katie wish she had a little makeup on herself right about now.

Jealousy slammed into her so quickly, she sat up and was almost across the space to rip the woman's arms off Jason's knee.

"Ohi kalo." Strong hands pushed her back down.

"Katie, lay still, we're at the hospital. Sit still so the doctor can look at you."

Then she noticed the blood dripping down his forehead and tried again to get across to him.

"Jason! You're bleeding."

"Yes, Airlea is just about to stitch me up," he said in a low voice. She watched as the pretty woman pulled out a very large needle and got it ready for him. Katie looked at Jason just as his eyes focused on the needle. He turned white and passed out, falling backward onto the bed.

Laughing at Jason's one weakness, she pushed the doctor's hands away.

"I'm okay," she tried to tell them, but she was forced back down on the pillows. Her stomach rolled a little, but for the most part, she felt fine.

Forty minutes later, she watched as Jason started waking up. She sat in a chair next to his bed in a private room and smiled as his eyes focused on her.

"Well, if this was your way of trying to ditch a girl after sleeping with her, there are better ways."

"What?" He shook his head and quickly grabbed it with a moan.

"Oh, no, you shouldn't move around. You have a very nasty concussion. They want to keep you overnight. They told me you might feel ill, so here's a bedpan." She handed it to him and watched as his color turned a little greenish. She walked over and rubbed his back as he proceeded to vomit into the pan.

"You're very lucky, you know," she said a few minutes later, as he leaned back and closed his eyes. "The doctor took x-rays and assured me that there is only a small chance you'll have major brain damage." She tried for humor and smiled when his eyes flew open.

"Oh, haha." He closed his eyes again. "Can you do anything about those bright lights? And maybe find me some mouthwash?"

She walked over and grabbed a small cup that Airlea had left for just this instance. She watched as Jason rinsed his mouth.

"Anything else?"

He looked at her. "Yeah, don't leave this room."

"I won't, there's a police officer just outside the door. They called them after you explained what happened. I've spent the last half an hour recapping what you told them. Only I can't remember anything, so they want to talk to you in the morning."

"Good." He leaned back and closed his eyes again. She went over and tried to dim the lights but ended up just turning them off instead. Then she walked over and said, "Scoot over, I'm coming up there with you." When he did, she slipped off her shoes and lay down next to him, putting her head on his shoulder.

"Thank you," she whispered.

"For what?"

"For saving us." She closed her eyes and listened to his heartbeat as he slept.

$\mathcal{B}$y the next morning, Katie felt almost human again. Since they'd lost both their backpacks back at the barn, the hospital had provided a change of clothing for them. Jason's pants were too short, and his shirt looked like it had been popular in the eighties, but they had showered and were both smelling a great deal better than they had yesterday.

Airlea had come in and checked on Jason through the night. Katie had actually ended up talking to the woman for several hours and by morning, her opinion of her had changed.

Katie was quick to judge people and sometimes had to admit that she was wrong about certain types of women.

Gorgeous, busty, raven-haired beauties tended to put Katie on edge. Airlea was different; she was so kind. During the night, Airlea had helped Katie with some Greek and Katie had helped her with some English. They'd laughed and at one point, Katie had explained everything that had happened to them over the last few days. Airlea had hung on every word as if she'd actually gone through everything herself.

It was the first time Katie had felt like she wasn't being judged by who she was related to. Actually, Katie didn't even think Airlea knew her full name. If she did, she didn't hint at it and that was just fine by Katie.

She found out that Airlea wasn't an Emergency room nurse like Katie had thought. Instead, she was a physical therapist for children. The young boy, Michael, had been her patient.

"You wouldn't know to look at him, but this time last year, Michael couldn't walk or speak. He'd been abused so much by his father that he'd been in a coma for two months."

Katie's heart broke a little for the young boy. Then Airlea smiled. "But he is doing well now and has told me he wishes to be a doctor when he grows up. With the help of the hospital and a new program we started, he might get his wish fulfilled."

That was when Katie realized she'd been wrong about the woman. Airlea had even helped Katie fill out and file the paperwork to get their replacement passports.

"Usually it takes twenty-four hours, but I know someone who can push it through quickly. Hopefully, they will be ready by tomorrow."

"That would be wonderful. We really do need to get to Italy as quickly as possible." Katie was going to miss her new friend when they left.

She had tried to get some more sleep that night, but every time they came to check up on Jason, she just found herself not able to fall back asleep. Jason, however, had pain pills that kept him blissfully snoring for most of the night.

At nine the next morning, the police arrived to take Jason's statement. The two young officers tried to explain what they could do for them, but after they left, Jason and Katie both knew there wasn't anything they could really do. After all, they had a good description of the men, but nothing else. Jason did know their names, Mikolas and Raul, but the police officer told them that they were very popular names in Greece. If Jason had gotten a license plate number or their last names it would have been more helpful.

"I couldn't even see their faces clearly at that point."

Katie realized what kind of pain he must have been in, running through the streets, carrying her over his shoulders. She looked at him now and could see he was almost back to his old self. His coloring had returned, and his eyes were back to their sparkly, light blue color. Yesterday, they'd been dull, and she knew he'd been in a great amount of pain.

The doctors released them and Airlea told them where they could find everything they needed for the remainder of their journey, including the ATM and American Embassy.

"My friend says that you just need to answer a few questions to get your temporary replacements. It shouldn't take long. Just ask for her at the front desk."

Airlea had given them her friend's business card.

When they left the hospital the first stop they made was to the ATM, where Katie pulled out a credit card and proceeded to get enough cash for ferry tickets to Italy, some new clothes, food, and anything else that might come up.

"Where did you hide that?" Jason asked, leaning against the ATM. He had a large bruise and a big knot on his forehead and looked damn sexy. The medicine the doctors had given him was easily taking care of the splitting headache he had.

His forehead had been covered with a white, square bandage earlier, but after leaving the hospital, it had been the first thing he'd discarded. His blue eyes sparkled again, and she could tell that he was feeling a little better.

"I have an inside pocket on my pants that I've been keeping this in, just for emergencies."

"Well, thank God for that. I didn't want to have to call your family and ask for money to get us to Rome." Upon hearing about her family, her cheerful attitude darkened.

"Don't."

"You know," she turned on him, "have I told you how annoying it is that you know me so well?"

He pulled her close. "Kat, it's because I know you so well that I can tell that at the mere mention of your family, you get upset and start over-thinking everything." He kissed her on the forehead as they started to walk to their next stop.

They walked into the US Embassy to get their replacement passports, making sure to ask for Airlea's friend. After almost four hours of answering more questions than they could count, they left with temporary replacement passports. Upon leaving the embassy, they were swarmed by news stations that had obviously heard that she was there. She kept her head down and a tight hold on Jason's arm. There were so many flashes from the cameras, she swore it took her half an hour to see normally again.

They fought the crowd and finally hailed a cab, which drove them to the small row of shops that Airlea had assured them would have some great clothing shops, as well as a place to get a decent meal and buy their ferry tickets.

She hated dealing with the press. They somehow made her feel inadequate and inferior, almost like she was back in high school, being judged by everyone. She knew the news of her being free would, no doubt, reach all the corners of the globe by nightfall.

"I hate reporters." The simple statement made Jason smile.

"Well, at least the news will clear up that you are indeed a free woman."

She turned, and crossing her arms, looked at him with question and laughter in her eyes.

It dawned on him what he had said, "No – not like that." She watched his face turn a light shade of red. "I mean that you weren't kidnapped." She could tell he was struggling to explain himself.

"It is so much fun to mess with you, Jason." She smiled and started walking towards a large shop that had clothes in the window.

"We could use the reporters to our advantage, you know."

Katie stopped and looked at him.

"Katie, you're in the spotlight, and if you remain so no one will try to grab you again."

"No, I don't want to be in the spotlight. I can't stand being in the spotlight. Spotlight! More like microscope. No." Shaking her head, she continued walking. "Besides, I think we've lost them."

She smiled at him.

He stopped her just outside the store. "You know how I took it, how I was after my father died. You could see my mood swings before they happened. Why won't you let me be here for you, the way you were there for me?"

She sobered up and looked at him. "Jason, my mother didn't die in some huge plane crash. She wasn't taken away from me quickly and tragically. No, my mother chose to lie to everyone who loved her for years, twenty-six years to be exact. It wasn't just a one-time lie; she continued to go behind our backs and live a double life. Being married to two men, raising two different families. Who does that?"

"Men, usually." She knew he was trying for humor, but the moment was gone.

"You know what?" She turned to walk into the shop. "You're right."

As they started shopping, she looked over at him and continued the conversation. "If it had been my father, I don't think it would have received as much news hype as it did. But because it was Kathleen Derby, socialite, they flooded the news every day with every aspect of our lives. Then, everyone, I trusted betrayed me to any network that would pay them enough." She flipped through the racks of clothes, looking for shirts and pants as he did the same across the aisle in the men's section. "Well, I handled that, but then I saw you." She stopped and looked off into the distance. He walked over to her, took her by the shoulders, and just looked into her eyes.

"Katie?" His voice snapped her out of the deep thought.

"What is your relationship with Katie Derby?" she asked.

He looked down at her with question in his eyes.

"What is your relationship with Katie Derby?" she asked again, pulling away from him slightly.

"Wait, what is this all about?"

"What is your relationship with Katie Derby?" she repeated a little louder.

"Katie, please." He looked around the small shop and noticed the sales clerk was staring at them, strangely.

"It's a simple question, Jason. One I've been waiting over a year to hear the answer to."

"Is that why you left?"

"No!" She tried to push him away.

"Katie," he held her still and looked into her eyes, "you are my best friend. You're the little girl I've loved since I rescued you from the swimming pool, the one person who's been there for me no matter what. The girl that's grown into a woman I love for so many reasons I couldn't possibly list them all in one lifetime."

Part of her broke off and floated to the heavens upon hearing his words. She looked into his blue eyes and thought of how perfect the moment was.

"Jason --" Just then the clerk walked up and interrupted, spoiling the most perfect moment in her life, so they continued shopping in complete silence.

Changing clothes in the dressing rooms, they packed

133

their other clothing purchases in the backpacks they had each bought.

They stopped by two other stores in the shopping area where they each bought flashlights, batteries, and baby wipes. Katie watched as Jason purchased a box of condoms, which had her heart fluttering the entire time they'd eaten lunch at the busy courtyard. They actually enjoyed a hamburger and French fries and watched people rushing around them.

"It's so nice to get American food somewhere." Jason bit into the large burger.

Katie watched in amusement as she nibbled on her chicken strips and fries.

After lunch, they walked to the middle of the mall area and purchased ferry tickets at a kiosk. The ferry was set to leave in just over two hours, which gave them plenty of time to walk the three blocks to the ferry docks.

Jason wanted to get there early, just in case, they ran into trouble. So they did a little more shopping, hitting some of the smaller, more local shops on the way to the docks. Both of them kept their eyes opened, looking for either man, never losing sight of each other. Actually, he'd held onto her hand and hadn't let go; she hadn't wanted him to.

They finally walked the short distance through the newer part of town and arrived at the docks. Jason was totally on guard now, watching everything. They boarded the boat from the very large dock area, quickly and without incident. She did notice the extra police around and wondered if they had anything to do with the men not being around, or if they had just given up trying to kidnap them.

They quickly found their small, private cabin on the large boat and locked themselves in, ready for the almost ten-hour trip to Italy. Katie looked across the space at the small bunks they each sat on and felt more nervous than she had ever felt around him.

It reminded her of her first kiss. She'd been at a friend's party, and they'd played spin the bottle. Whoever the bottle landed on, they would have to go into the closet with and kiss.

Of course, she'd hoped that it would land on Jason, so they wouldn't have to do anything, or so her eleven-year-old mind had told her. But no, it had landed on Dave. Dave had been the boy who'd hit puberty before all the others. His hormones were in full swing and she'd nervously entered the closet where he'd instantly kissed her, pushing his tongue into her mouth. He'd tasted of Cheetos and Root Beer, a mix that still to this day turned her off.

Now she sat on one of the bunks and felt the room getting smaller, and the air somehow seemed to be leaving the space as well. She wasn't nervous like she'd been with Dave; this was a different kind of nervousness. It was more anxious than anything. She knew what it was like to be with Jason. He was Jason, her best friend, her only lover, yet all of a sudden, she didn't know what to say to him. How to act around him. She was probably over-thinking things again.

She looked over at him and her eyes took in the bump and bruise on his forehead, then followed the path down his jaw and his neck. She noticed how wide his shoulders were and remembered how they felt above her as she grabbed them and held them to her. She watched his arms flex and remembered how they felt holding her. Her eyes traveled down his arms and she looked at his hands, remembering how they felt on her skin, how they had caused her to moan and squirm under his light touch. Then she went back to his chest and remembered nibbling on his nipples and licking his stomach muscles, following the light trail of hair down to his cock, remembering what he did with it and how she'd enjoyed sucking him to completion. She couldn't take her eyes off his crotch and was mesmerized by every movement he made. She could see him getting hard under his jeans and couldn't stop herself from licking her lips with desire.

Jason watched Katie and knew she was nervous and was probably over-thinking their relationship. What did she have to be nervous about? Then she looked down at his hands and he realized she was not just nervous, she was turned on by him. He watched her eyes travel his body and couldn't stop himself from getting hard. How could she do this to him by just looking at him?

Smiling to himself, he leaned back and thought about having a little fun with her. If she could make him feel this way, he was going to show her just how much he could turn her on in return. Slowly, he pulled his arms over his head and gripped the back of his neck, showing off his perfectly toned arms. The motion stretched his new shirt over his chest and pecs, giving her a very nice view of his build.

He watched in amazement as her eyes followed his every movement and then she zeroed in on his arms and chest. He slumped a little in his seat and spread his legs wide, almost bumping into her knees. Her eyes went to his jean-clad legs and then moved up to his crotch, where it was obvious that he wanted her, too.

He watched as her eyes grew large and her tongue darted out and licked her bottom lip.

"Katie." When he spoke, her eyes darted to his like she'd been caught with her hand in the cookie jar. "Come over here." He told himself that he'd give her a choice, but the truth was, he didn't know what he'd do if she told him no.

Without saying anything, she stood and walked the two steps it took to cross the small space. She sat next to him, and as he reached his hands out to touch her, her head dropped back, and her eyes closed. Lightly he traced her neck and ran his thumb over her bottom lip to feel the moisture there from her tongue. She took his thumb into her mouth and lightly sucked on it, and he felt a jolt of electricity that traveled all the way to his core, as she sucked on it. When she smiled up at him, there was so much seduction steaming off her skin that he became nervous as well.

He moved his hands lower to her shoulders, then gently pulled her shirt buttons loose one at a time, until she sat before him, exposed to his view in broad daylight.

She'd purchased some fancy new bra and panty sets and when she'd bought them, he'd only had one thing in mind -- getting them off her slowly.

Pulling her shirt off her shoulders, he made eye contact again with her. They hadn't kissed yet and the anticipation was almost too much, but he wanted it to last a while longer.

Pushing her legs wide, he ran his hands up and down

her new jeans and watched as her eyes clouded over. Unbuttoning, unzipping, and removing her layers undid his willpower. He felt his hands shake as he helped her step out of her jeans. She stood before him clad only in bright pink silk and lace and he wished for a camera to hold onto this moment forever.

The boat had already left the dock and the light was changing, growing softer in the cabin, casting shadows and giving off hues of color that highlighted her beauty.

"You are too beautiful," he whispered.

He watched as heat flooded into her face and he could tell she was becoming shy. Slowly, for her pleasure, he reached up and removed his shirt as she stood in front of him. Once his shirt was tossed aside, he stood and removed his jeans just as slowly. Her eyes followed his every movement and he wished he could hear her thoughts.

Now he stood in front of her, clad only in his new cotton boxers and felt almost out of control. The shaking had increased and so had his need.

"Jason…" He watched as she started to raise her hand towards him. "You are so beautiful, so strong. I can't believe you want me."

"My God, Kat, if you knew how long I've wanted you, wanted this." He stepped closer, closing the distance and took her into his arms. Her skin felt so soft next to his and he ran his hands up and down her back slowly. His mouth hovered just over hers, "I want you so bad, I can barely breathe through it."

Then he was kissing her, and her hands were on him, all over him, until his eyes closed and he moaned.

Backing them up, he quickly pulled the couch down so

that it became a double bed, then he gently laid her down and covered her with his body.

She tasted and smelled so good as he ran soft kisses down her neck until he reached the pink silk that covered her. He bent down to wet it with his mouth until he felt her nipple peeking through the light material. He pulled it aside and just looked at her; she was perfection.

Running kisses along her collarbone, he repeated the motion on the other side, then removed the barrier altogether. Next, he ran kisses down her tight stomach and played his tongue just around her navel until she was squirming under him.

"What?" He laughed at her obvious frustration. "Tell me what you want, I want to hear you tell me everything."

At first, he thought she was going to turn shy and keep quiet, but she surprised him when she started talking dirty, telling him exactly what she wanted him to do to her.

He smiled and followed her every demand, running his mouth over the outside of her panties until they, too, were wet. He slid them down her legs and took her with his mouth until she moaned with delight, then he moved back up her body and slid slowly into her as they both moaned.

This time was different, this time they could see each other, what they did to one another. He knew he'd never get the vision of Katie out of his mind, laying on the cushions, her hair fanned out, and her eyes clouded with desire.

Later that night, they dressed and traveled to the dining area and enjoyed the large buffet that was offered. They sat at the table and she looked across to him and flirted with him, almost like he'd done to her in the cabin. She made a point to lick the whipped cream from her mocha off her fingers slowly, enjoying the heat that came into his eyes.

She ran her foot up his leg under the table, something she'd seen in a movie once, and had always wanted to try. His eyes had bulged, and his smile had been devious. She could tell he was thinking of everything he could do to her when they got back to their cabin, and she could feel herself quivering in anticipation.

Would there ever be a time when she didn't want him like she wanted him now? Her mind flashed to a memory of seeing him naked for the first time in full light and she felt herself getting wet. Just the thought of him naked, standing in front of her, did this to her.

She'd always admired his body. He had taken Judo at the country club while she'd attended gymnastic classes, something her mother had forced her to do. She'd always hated bending and jumping about. She'd wanted to be a dancer instead, but her mother had quickly told her she was too short, and her legs weren't long enough. So, she'd attended gymnastics against her wishes. She couldn't complain now, though. At twenty-four she was more flexible than most girls and she knew it had come in handy with Jason. She smiled and remembered what they'd done just before coming to grab some food.

"What?" he smiled across from her.

"What," she replied back with her sexiest voice.

"You know you are in so much trouble now, don't you?"

She smiled and enjoyed how quickly he paid for their meal and started pulling her back down the hallway towards their cabin, with her laughing the entire way down the long hallway.

When he finally got the door open after fumbling with the key, he pushed her into the dark room and threw her up against the back of the door, his mouth on hers and his hands everywhere. He tasted like spice and she couldn't get enough of his hands on her. The skirt she'd been wearing was hiked up and her new panties yanked down quickly. Then his fingers were inside her and her nails dug into his shoulders as she held on.

He fumbled for his zipper and a condom and before she knew what was happening, he'd grabbed her legs and was thrusting deep inside her. She held onto his shoulders as he took her quickly against the locked door.

His face was set in concentration and so she reached up to grab his head and bring it to hers, taking his lips between her teeth and nibbling just a little until he moaned, and she could feel him buck under her hands. His thrust became uneven and when she reached around to hold his butt, she knew he'd lost it just as she had. He buried his face in her hair and felt his warm breath on her neck. She didn't want to move, couldn't move. Her legs were shaking, and she wasn't sure that if she opened her eyes, she would see anything. How could sex destroy you so fast? He'd turned her into a marshmallow, soft and gooey and easily melted.

Jason surprised her by picking her up in his arms in a quick motion, then depositing her gently on the narrow bed. He disposed of his shoes quickly and climbed in next to her.

"You destroyed me," he said into her hair again as he spooned her.

She laughed, "Really? I was just thinking the same thing about you."

"Katie…" He snuggled deeper into her back, running his hand over her naked thigh. "I'm really glad I came to Europe to save you."

"Me, too." With that, she heard him snoring and she smiled into the darkness until sleep finally overcame her.

CHAPTER 10

When the ferry docked in Brindisi, Italy, early the next morning, he could tell Katie was a bundle of nerves, no doubt anxious about meeting her family. Jason's eyes scanned the docks, searching for the men who were looking for them. He had the funny feeling they had somehow made the journey to Italy, as well.

Whoever had hired the men hadn't spared any expenses; the cargo van had been brand new. He had a few questions about how the men had been able to stay on their trail. Katie had come up with an idea last night, that they must have left some sort of tracking device in her backpack when it had been left at the café, and that's how they had tracked them down in the barn.

There was no way they had just stumbled upon them in a barn in a large field in the middle of nowhere. There was no way they had gotten that lucky.

He didn't worry about being tracked anymore since they had both lost their phones. Well, lost everything actually. And they hadn't even called her family to update them on their progress, so nobody knew where they were yet. He wanted to keep it that way.

He knew that the other men were watching the airports in Rome and thought about taking a train instead but knew that the train and bus stations might be watched as well. He just couldn't chance it.

So, they'd walked into the car rental place with freshly dispensed cash from the ATM across town and rented a small sedan.

It was less than a six-hour drive to Rome, but Jason knew they weren't going to be taking the shortest route. He had mapped out a route on the car's dash GPS which he thought might throw anyone off their trail. Instead of taking the most direct route, diagonal across the land, they were going to take the east route and head north until just past Pescara, then head southwest into Rome.

After they had packed up their backpacks into the compact sedan, he started driving out of town. He was happy driving, he enjoyed taking the less-traveled roads that wound around the little villages. Taking the back streets meant that several times they would hit dead ends that the GPS didn't show or streets that were too narrow for cars to pass through.

But they enjoyed every minute and Katie couldn't stop talking about how different Italy was then Greece. Here, everything just seemed... shinier -- her words, not his.

It's almost as if she'd come alive. She sat on the edge of her seat, taking in everything and talking about the buildings and people they passed.

The scenery was flatter here than in Greece but still seemed more beautiful. It seemed more populated, the roads and towns better maintained. Plus, there seemed to be tourists everywhere. In Greece, he could only see signs of tourism in the larger cities, whereas here, even in the smaller ocean-side towns, people were enjoying the beaches and small-town scenery.

They stopped in a small town just off the waterfront for lunch and dined at a cafe in Via Molise. They sat on the street patio and ate the best pizza they'd ever had, as they watched people coming and going at the local shops. Italy felt different to him as well. Things looked cleaner, shinier, as Katie had said. The tourists seemed happier and more relaxed, almost as if they weren't rushed. Plus, the locals looked healthier and happier. The houses were better maintained and there were quite a few more of them. There were also many more towns here. The population here seemed triple what it had been in Greece.

He could smell the ocean and when they finished lunch, they decided to take a break from riding in the car.

They held hands as they slowly made their way the few blocks to the beach, where they watched people play in the Mediterranean under the warm sun.

The water and white sands looked so inviting that Katie had removed her clothes and shoes and waded in wearing the swimsuit she'd purchased just yesterday. Jason finally broke down and pulled off his shirt and shoes and followed her into the cool water with just his shorts on. In the last year, he had never felt this wonderful or this relaxed. He enjoyed holding onto Katie in the surf, holding her wet body next to his, and he thought about the excitement of taking her then and there in the cool water, but there were too many people around. He really enjoyed the feel of her wet body next to his; maybe they would have to take a shower later that night.

He thought they would have to make it back down this way once things settled down, so they could spend more time on the white sandy beaches. After almost an hour of playing in the warm surf, he knew they needed to head out. Dusting the sand off was easy since they had both dried off during the short walk back to the rental car. They shook as much sand off as they could and started out of town. They took the scenic route along the water's edge for a while, and Katie stared off into the water.

"I wouldn't mind living here."

He smiled; he was thinking the same thing. Really, they didn't have anything or anyone to go back to the States for. He could easily get a job anywhere. He still had a few credits before he could officially take the bar exam, but he could look into taking Italy's equivalent and start his own practice here. Thinking on it, he silently watched the scenery pass by.

A few hours later, they made the turnoff to start heading west towards Rome. Most of the houses here were large, white stucco buildings with red, tiled roofs surrounded by acres of large fields and rolling hills. She told him that she had enjoyed seeing all the different countries during her year abroad, but that this place felt different. He agreed. He'd enjoyed their travels and the only thing that could have possibly made it better was if they'd done them together, instead of him following her, out of sight.

He started thinking of the meeting ahead of them. Of her seeing her mother, fathers, and brothers. He'd known Rodrick and Kathleen all his life, he'd always looked up to the couple. After Jason's father had died, Rodrick had taken him under his wing. He'd always known he could count on the man. He looked to Ric like he was a brother, something he'd never had the privilege of having himself. His mother and Kathleen had always been in the same circles. They'd attended all the events at the country club together. One year, the families had even vacationed together in Puerto Rico. He knew Rodrick and Ric felt hurt about Kathleen's deception, and to be honest, he had as well. He'd taken it very personally, at first. After all, she'd lied to him as well. But after meeting with her and hearing her side of things, he just couldn't stay mad. People made mistakes in life. After all, he wasn't perfect, and he didn't expect others to be either.

"It's almost as if I can feel the history in my blood coming alive." Katie interrupted his thoughts, and she looked at him as he smiled over at her. "It's hard to explain, even the smells are just… right." She looked over at Jason and realized he was quiet, almost too quiet.

"What's going on?" She leaned against the door and watched him drive the windy road.

"Hmm?"

"You. You're awful quiet."

"Just enjoying the drive, enjoying you." He flipped on the wiper blades as a light rain started to hit the windshield. Somehow the rain made the field even greener. He could make out a light rainbow and silently wished she'd change the subject.

"I'm not buying it." She crossed her arms over her chest.

"You know," his smile faded, knowing how determined Katie was, "she's going to be there."

"Oh! I knew you were thinking about something. I just hoped it was something other than her."

He chuckled, "You say *her* like it's a curse word."

"It is in my book." She propped up her feet on the dash and crossed her arms, then looked out the window. He could tell she was trying to avoid this conversation.

"Katie, you're going to have to deal with her at some point in your life. What about your brother and his new wife? Are you just planning to never spend family holidays together? And do you ever want to meet your brother Dante?"

"I don't know. I was going to start with meeting my BD first, then see where it led." She pouted and looked out the window, quietly.

"Well, at least that's a start. You have heard that they are together right? They married again shortly after your parents' divorce was final."

She had; it had been all over the news. Her mother had finally, twenty-six years too late in her book divorced her father and had moved to Rome to be with Damiano Cardone.

"Why do you think I was meeting him in Greece?"

He laughed, "Well, I know she's been worried about you since the day you took off. She was on her way there, you know."

"Where?" Katie sat up and looked at him.

"To Boston, to see you."

"What?" This was news to her. The last she'd heard from her mother was a quick call which had interrupted a very awkward conversation with Jason.

"She showed up right after I got back to your place and started looking for you. I knew you'd taken your passport and wallet but had left some major items behind. Like the iPhone, I bought you for Christmas."

He looked sad and she felt bad that she'd forgotten the damn phone.

"Sorry, I wasn't thinking clearly."

"I figured that, since you had also taken a pair of shoes I knew you hated and left your comfy clothes behind."

"You really do know me that well." She thought for the first time in over a year about all the items she'd left behind. "Where is all my stuff?"

He looked over at her and smiled. "Storage."

"Good, that's good. I'd hate to see all my Gucci bags go to Goodwill and sell for a dollar, or worse, go to that blond girl down the hall from me." They both laughed.

A few hours later, they drove into Rome. The evening traffic was heavy, and she was very tired of sitting in the car. She didn't know what the plans were, where they were going to stay, but she knew she wasn't in the mood to meet any of her family tonight.

"How about we stop and get dinner and a hotel." She was surprised the thought came from Jason since she'd just been thinking the same thing.

"You read my mind."

Less than an hour later, they found a wonderful bed and breakfast and lucked out that the place had a cancellation for the night. It was a beautiful old brick building right across from the Colosseum. Third Floor Bed and Breakfast, the antique sign read.

When they got to their room, he opened the curtains and they both gasped at the beautiful sight of the Colosseum out their window. They couldn't have asked for a better, more romantic room. After dropping off their bags, they decided to spend the rest of the evening pretending to be tourists. Actually, they really *were* tourists, since neither of them had ever been to Rome before.

They walked across the street, hand in hand, and enjoyed going around the Colosseum for almost an hour. They even joined a tour group, learning the history of the Colosseum and watching several of the plays and skits that were going on around the building. When he pulled her close in a dark stone hallway of the underground Colosseum walkways and kissed her, she would have sworn she felt the whole building vibrate with her.

Then they walked over to the Arch of Constantine. It was a lot larger than Katie had thought. She'd seen it on several movies and never imagined all the detail that could still be seen seventeen centuries later.

They had purchased a disposable camera and had taken plenty of pictures of each other along the way. At the Archway, Jason asked a woman to take a few pictures of them standing under the archway. He'd quickly kissed her for one, and in the other, they'd smiled at each other. She couldn't wait to have the film developed and silently wished for her iPhone and its digital photo abilities.

From there they walked over to the Temple of Venus, where Jason bought her a small trinket from one of the many carts that lined the streets. The bracelet had the image of Venus, the goddess of love and bringer of good fortune, or so the salesman said in broken English.

"It suits you." He took his time putting it on her wrist. For a small, cheap trinket, Katie held the gift dear to her heart.

By this time the sun was setting, and they ended their tour of Rome back at the Colosseum, watching the sun sink low behind the large walls, lighting the sky in a spectacular array of light and colors.

Tourists clapped their hands when the sun finally dropped below the great walls, leaving everyone in its shadows. She pulled Jason's head down and kissed him to more cheers from people around them. Laughing, they walked back to a cafe just down the street from where they were staying and ate dinner under the stars, with the street lights blinding her to anything else but him.

She never imagined being with him like this. She looked across the table and noticed that the bruising on his face had disappeared almost completely. She knew that he still had to have the small stitches, which sat just under two white butterfly bandages under his longer hair, removed. But his face was back to normal and he had never looked as good as he did sitting across from her in the most romantic setting she'd ever witnessed. Her mind quickly turned to the pleasure she was imagining under his hands. How had it come to this? Was she always going to be thinking about having his hands on her?

Looking across the table at him, she saw him smile at her and she could tell he was thinking almost the same thing as she was.

"If you keep looking at me like that..." he let the statement drop off.

"What? Will you punish me? Spank me? Maybe I want you to spank me. Maybe I want you to punish me." She didn't know where all that had come from, but when she saw his eyes cloud over, she knew she was in for it, and her excitement doubled.

"Check!" Jason raised his hand and waved at the waiter.

After paying, he took her hand and they walked quickly towards the bed and breakfast. They made it back to their room, but barely. They were both breathless when they came together behind their room door, and she knew it had nothing to do with the two flights of steep stairs they had just climbed.

His hot mouth melted her control and he held her against the wall until she pushed him and reversed their positions, almost knocking down a picture from the wall. Now his back was against the door and she enjoyed watching his amusement at her boldness. She nibbled his lip and ran her hands over him quickly.

"Little rough, aren't you?" he asked, and she answered him by taking his bottom lip between her teeth and nibbling on it. Then she was pushing his hands away from trying to untuck her shirt. She stood back and slowly unbuttoned her blouse, almost making a show out of it, removing it slowly. Then she followed it with her skirt until finally, she stood in her sexy black bra and panties in front of him.

He stood there, leaning against the door, breathless.

"My God, you are beautiful."

Walking slowly towards him, she removed his shirt in one fast motion. He was sure she'd popped a few buttons, but he didn't care. Then she quickly removed his belt and started in on his jeans.

"Katie?"

"Don't! Let me," she moaned as she started trailing kisses down his chest until she hit the top of his jeans.

Then she pulled them over his hips and smiled as he groaned her name.

She wasn't going to let him control the speed this time.

This time she was in charge and wanted, more than anything, to see him squirm under her hands and mouth. She wanted to show him that she could be in charge, that she could give him as much pleasure as he'd shown her the last few days.

She slowly pulled his jeans down his legs and watched as his arousal pushed against his skin-tight boxer's briefs. Then, slowly, she freed him and held her breath at how beautiful he was. She reached for him and ran a finger up and down his length, enjoying the fact that he held his breath as he watched her face.

"Let me know if I do something you don't like," she whispered.

Then, as she watched his face, she leaned in and kissed him, then licked the trail her finger had just taken. He grabbed her head and moaned, so she continued to experiment with her mouth, giving him pleasure and arousing herself at the same time.

"Katie," he said, then he grabbed her under her arms and hauled her up. Taking the dozen or so steps to the large four-poster bed, he dropped her on the soft mattress and was inside her before she could think.

He held himself above her, looking into her eyes until finally, she grabbed his hips and forced him to move.

"Please, Jason, I need you."

"I need you, too, Katie, too damn much." Then he was moving quickly, and his thrusts became almost violent as they were both overwhelmed by each other.

The next morning, they decided it was time to finally call

her family. It had taken him quite a bit to convince her that they needed the extra help in figuring out who was after her. Plus, they needed to find out where to meet everyone.

She would have been happy continuing on her travels until she became tired of it all and returned home to Boston. But Jason had convinced her that a trip to meet Damiano Cardone was the next move they needed to make.

After the call to both her fathers, it was agreed the best place to meet would be at the New Edges Corporate office building, which happened to be only a few blocks away.

They checked out of the B&B and left their bags in the rental car, which they decided to leave parked in a small spot they had hunted down the day before. Then they set off on foot for the short journey.

They stopped and ate breakfast and had some coffee at one of the street cafes. Watching people walk by was one of the normal things Katie missed about being in larger cities.

When they were done eating, they still had an hour before the meeting, so they spent the time walking around the stores and enjoying the scenery. Then they started heading to the larger office building they could see in the distance. The tall glass tower was a beacon in the older city with its large, bright sign that hung above the rest of the shorter, older buildings. The closer they got to the building, the more nervous Katie felt. She actually felt her hands sweat and they even shook a little.

She knew Jason understood her and he tried multiple times to keep her mind off the meeting. He joked with her, trying to get her to think and talk about other things, but nothing was working. He'd always had a knack of keeping her mind off impending doom. Back in high school, he'd joked and made her laugh right before every test she'd had. Then he'd been there to help pick her up if she had failed or help her celebrate if she had passed. He, of course, had always gotten A's, no matter what class. She had struggled a little more in school. It didn't help that she had no clue what she wanted to do after school. She'd gone through multiple career plans. Doctor, teacher, architect, lawyer, and even, at one time, a zoologist.

Jason had always known what he wanted to be; law had been in his blood. All his hard work at school was paying off. When she'd left, he was on his last year of college.

Now, however, she couldn't stop thinking about what was about to happen. They were just across the street from the large building. She wanted to turn and run, with or without Jason, but then he reached over and grabbed her hand and she felt her nerves disappear.

"I'll be right here with you." He smiled over at her just as they heard the squeals of tires.

"They are at New Edges, you fool. How could you let her get this close?"

"We know; we've been waiting for her here. We're right outside; don't worry, we've got her."

"Fine, just take care of it, and don't mess up this time."

The line went dead, and he cursed and tossed the phone down. "Okay, Raul, we need to do this quick. Don't screw it up or we'll be out of our money."

❄

Rodrick Derby sat in the lobby of New Edges next to his son, Ric. The fact that he was on enemy territory didn't escape his attention. But he'd do anything for his kids. And no matter what Kathleen had said or done, nobody and nothing could take Katie away from him.

She was his daughter. After all, he'd been the one who had picked her up after a spill on her bike, he'd been the one who'd been there for her her whole life, whether she'd been ill, sad, or happy.

It had cut him deep, at first, when Katie hadn't called him this last year. But he knew his daughter, knew that she needed time to heal. He couldn't blame her for taking off. After all, it's what she'd been taught to do. Every time he and Kathleen had problems in the past, they would retreat to different corners of the globe. He to Alaska on his extended fishing trips and her to Italy. Now he knew why she had always frequented here. The two main reasons were walking towards him now.

Seeing Damiano and Dante Cardone walk out of the glass elevators did little to calm his nerves as he waited for his daughter. The lobby of the building was fairly packed since there were small shops on the first two floors.

They stood, and Ric shook both men's hands, though Rodrick did not. Ric had been the first to figure out his connection with Dante. They'd worked together in Portland and he had noticed the resemblance. The connection hadn't come to light until Ric had confronted his mother and forced Kathleen's hand. Then she had called him to confess when he was on vacation in Alaska. It had been a call that he had thought had ruined his life.

But being afraid for Katie now had made Rodrick realize he didn't care if she wasn't his biological child, she was his in many more ways. He'd never been more afraid than when he'd received the ransom call at his new apartment in Portland. He'd moved there to be closer to his son. After all, he'd kind of been leaning on Ric for moral support in the last year. It had been a hard blow for them both to get over. Now Rodrick didn't give a damn about what Kathleen had done.

Looking across the room, he noticed how Katie resembled both men and his heart sank a little. It was true. Looking at them, he could tell that his daughter was a perfect match to their gene pool. She had her father's eyes, nose, hair, and coloring. Rodrick no longer cared about what his ex-wife had done to him, but he wanted to get his hands on her for all the years she had lied to his daughter.

He thought of Katie, how she'd always been a daddy's girl. Looking over at Damiano, he wondered what her life would have been like with him. Would she have been a daddy's girl with him, too?

"I understand that under the circumstances this is a very unusual meeting," Damiano said in a very thick accent. "Our only concern is for the girl's safety. Kathleen has decided to stay at home for this meeting. I'm sure Katie would like to meet her in a more private setting."

Rodrick almost laughed. If he knew his little girl, Katie would see her mother again when hell froze over. Then he realized, she truly was his girl; her feelings and attitude matched his so closely. She may not be his biologically, but she was his in every other way. He smiled to himself, knowing that he had made the best part of his daughter. He had actually been surprised that she had agreed to meet the

Cardones at all. But he supposed she couldn't hold her mother's past transgressions against someone she didn't know, much to his own thinking.

"I trust your trip was pleasant." Dante motioned for them to all sit again.

Just then there was a commotion and they watched in horror as a small truck crashed through the front doors, shattering glass, and sending people scattering in all directions.

Rodrick looked at the man driving the truck and recognized with horror that it was Jason slumped behind the wheel. Glass shards were everywhere around him and he was bleeding from the cuts to his face and hands, as the horn blasted continually. He looked around for his daughter as he rushed to Jason's side.

"Jason!" He shook the boy until he saw with relief that his eyes opened.

"They grabbed her, in the white van," Jason said.

Ric and Dante both looked up as a white van turned the corner at a very high speed. Then they looked at each other and took off running in the same direction.

Dante yelled, "I'll drive."

CHAPTER 11

*K*atie was fighting for her life. She remembered being grabbed off the street. The van hadn't even slowed down when arms had reached out and plucked her from the sidewalk. Jason's hand had been ripped from hers, almost yanking her arm out of its socket. She was pushed into the van and held down with a vile smelling white cloth over her mouth until darkness overcame her.

This time she didn't think she'd been out very long because she felt the vehicle jolt. Then she heard metal on metal and heard a horn blowing in the distance as they continued to drive.

The men didn't pay her any attention after the loud sounds, so she lay there unmoving with her eyes closed, thinking. She hoped they assumed she was still unconscious and listened for her opportunity, any opening she might have to jump into motion. The van traveled so fast that with every corner they took, she rolled with the motion.

They must have driven for half an hour before she felt the van slowing down. She lay there, unmoving until she heard the door open, then she cracked open her eyes and kicked the first person she saw in the groin. When he toppled over, she jumped from the van and started running away from the vehicle. She made it a few steps only to be grabbed from behind and tossed against the back of the van. Her head snapped back against the side of the van, causing her to bite the side of her mouth so hard that she tasted blood. her head hurt.

She faced the man whose nose was still crooked from the break Jason had given him over a week ago. Mikolas.

"What do you want?"

"Well, now, looks like she played opossum on us," he chuckled at the man who was still hunched over, holding his crotch. "Get up Raul, we have a job to do."

Katie watched in horror as the big man walked towards her with the same white cloth from earlier. Knowing that if he got it over her face again she might never wake up, she shouted,

"I can pay you!" She held herself ready for a fight.

The man stopped. "We are already getting paid," he said, and he started walking towards her again.

"I'll double it," she blurted out. Knowing she was just stalling, she tried to look around for any help. It looked like they were in the industrial part of town. She could see large warehouse buildings, and unfortunately, there wasn't anyone in sight. She knew that if she tried to take off on foot, they would just jump in the van and grab her again. She needed to get back to where there were people and she could only think of one way of doing that.

"Well, now," the man scratched his chin and looked

down at his partner, "that would make our take four hundred thousand each."

Katie tried not to show the shock on her face. Was someone willing to pay these men four hundred thousand to kidnap her? And do what? Kill her? Who wanted her dead or out of the way that badly?

She remembered the call from her family. Someone had demanded a ransom of ten million dollars. She knew that her father's business easily made that much. Even her biological father was probably worth that much, though she didn't know if they had called him and demanded money, as well. So whoever wanted her was trying to bleed her family out of their hard-earned money and she knew that her dad and brother would have gladly paid any price for her.

She had never really thought about her family's money that way before. Sure, growing up she had everything she ever needed, driven the nicest cars, had the finest clothes that she could ever possibly want, gone to the best schools. But she had her own money she had always used. For the past ten years, she'd only used her inheritance from her grandmother. She had invested it herself and she'd been smart enough with it that she had easily tripled the amount given to her.

But in the last year, she had hardly been spending any money at all, just paying for hotels and travel.

Now, after living the way she had been, she doubted that she would ever go back to the way she had lived before. There was something to be said about the simple life, and she'd grown accustomed to enjoying the simpler things in life.

She knew that her only possible chance of escape

would be to get them to a very public place, so she took a chance.

"Yes, I can easily pay you double." She reached into her pocket and pulled out her credit card. "Just get me to my bank."

Dante and Ric drove across town at high speeds, following the van. Ric was impressed at his half-brother's driving abilities.

"Don't worry, we will get her back. I know these streets very well," Dante said, as Ric held on to his seat. Dante took a turn quickly, trying to keep the van within sight.

All Ric could focus on was his sister -- seeing her again, hearing her laughter, having her joke with him. He just had to get her back. Images of her flashed before his eyes. Her as a child, with no front teeth, sitting in front of the Christmas tree. Her on her horse during a riding lesson. Her in her gymnastics outfit, bending and twirling her teenage body around. Her in her Prom dress as their mother took countless pictures. Then his mind flashed to the last time he'd seen her. She'd retreated to his place in Portland for spring break. He knew she'd been hiding from someone, most likely a boy. She'd nervously been checking her phone all week for messages. Then she'd left his place early to meet up with her girlfriends in Mexico. He'd never figured out what she'd been anxious about; he'd been too busy with his own problems then.

Now, he'd do anything to get that week back, to get his sister back. He didn't give a damn if she was his half-sister. He'd grown up with her under his heels his entire life. All he could remember was her being there.

He didn't want that to change, no matter what.

They followed the white van for almost twenty minutes before they lost it on the outskirts of the industrial park.

"Damn it!" Dante slammed his hand against his steering wheel. "Did you see where they went?"

"No, let's keep looking. They have to be here somewhere."

They looked around, scanning the small streets as Dante slowly drove by the last place they'd seen the van.

Dante could hardly breathe through the worry and fear he had for a sister he hadn't even met yet. Looking over at Ric, he knew the fear in him was most likely doubled since Ric and Katie had grown up together.

"Go back down that last street. I think I saw something." Ric pointed down a side street.

Dante turned his small Audi around in one quick turn and headed slowly back down the narrow street.

"Stop!" Ric shouted. Dante stopped the car and they both noticed a large, empty parking lot next to an old building. Katie and two large men stood just outside the white van. One of the men was hunched over on his knees, holding his crotch.

"That's our sister, kick them where it counts," Ric said, smiling.

Dante felt an enormous sense of pride knowing that his sister had probably kicked the man in the groin.

"I'm getting out here. I'll circle around and try to help her. Call the cops and tell them where we are. I don't know if they have weapons, but I need to stay out of sight until I do. I've been shot at once in my life and I don't intend to let that happen again. You need to come around and try to block that gate somehow." Ric pointed to a large fenced area. Dante noticed that the van would have to pass through it in order to leave the secured parking area.

Ric jumped out of Dante's car, shut the door quietly, then he ran off to circle the building.

Dante grabbed his cell phone and quickly called his father, relaying where they were and what was going on.

He watched as Katie argued with the larger man, and he hoped that she could keep them busy as he slowly moved his car to block the driveway with it.

He watched as the larger man grabbed Katie's arm and started walking her around to the front of the van, where he shoved her into the large door. Then the two men argued as the larger one pushed the smaller against the side of the vehicle. He watched as finally, they started to get back into the van.

The van pulled away and turned towards him. Dante sat there behind the wheel of his car and watched them drive closer. Where was Ric? What would he do if they stopped? When they were closer, the larger man finally saw Dante's car blocking their way out. In the split second, before Dante realized what was going to happen, he braced himself for the impact.

Ric got out of the car and started to sprint towards the side of the large brick building.

It seemed like just yesterday that he and Roberta had been the ones people were after. Now someone was after his baby sister and he damned well was going to make sure he got his hands on whoever was trying to hurt her.

Just then he heard a noise and watched the van start to drive away. Rushing back over towards the gate, he watched in horror as the van crashed violently into Dante's small Audi. It hit the driver's side with a loud bang, and glass and plastic flew into the air. The van backed up and proceeded to ram the small sedan until the roadway was clear, then it took off down the street. Knowing the Audi was beyond drivable, he watched in horror as his sister's face appeared in the back window. She did something then that surprised him; she held up her bank card in the back window and pointed to it.

Rushing over to the car, he silently prayed that his half-brother was still alive. The car was mangled beyond recognition. He rushed over to the driver's side and noticed that Dante sat with his seat belt still on. His head was rolled back, and his eyes were closed. Screaming his name, he opened the door.

Dante woke up to Ric yelling his. His left hip and shoulder were screaming with pain and his left leg sat at an odd angle.

"Did you get her?" Dante asked Ric.

"Oh, thank God! You're alive! No, damn it, they took off in the van after ramming your car out of the way, but I think I know where they're going. Katie held up her bank card in the back window as they drove off. I think they're taking her to the bank."

Dante watched as Ric reached across him and grabbed the cell phone that was sitting in the seat next to him.

"Dad?" Ric yelled while holding his hand on a large cut on Dante's leg, trying to stifle the bleeding, "No, they're heading to the bank. Katie held up her credit card. I think it was her International Bank Card. She was trying to tell us where they were going." He waited. "Yeah, okay, send an ambulance to our location. They rammed Dante's car – No, he's awake – broken leg, possibly his shoulder." His conversation was choppy, as he answered his father's questions.

"Don't worry about me," Dante said, trying to make his voice sound stronger than he felt. "Just get Katie."

"They're getting her, just relax, an ambulance is coming." Ric leaned over him and Dante felt more pressure on his hip until he almost screamed with pain.

"Sorry, I've got to stop the bleeding." Dante watched as his brother's face started to fade in front of his eyes, just before everything went black.

"I don't need a damn doctor. What I need is a car!" Jason said for the tenth time. When the men in the van had grabbed Katie, he'd jumped into a small truck, that someone was unloading supplies from a few feet away, and he had tried to follow the van. The short chase ended up with the larger vehicle ramming his into the front of the building.

"Just settle back, Jason," Rodrick said, pushing him back onto the leather couch in Damiano's large private office. "Ric and Dante took off after the van right after you crashed into the building. They're keeping us posted on my phone."

Rodrick turned to a very Italian man in a suit who'd been pacing the floor. "Damiano, just how long is it going to take for those police to get here?"

Jason looked at the man and realized this was Katie's BD, as she called him. He could instantly see the heritage. The man looked upset and scared, making Jason realize that he could scratch him off his suspect list. No way the man's nerves were faked. Whatever happened, Damiano had no part in what was happening to his daughter.

Just then, the man's cell phone rang. Jason was getting agitated, his head hurt, and he wanted desperately to be out there helping look for Katie.

"Hello – where? – Yes, I'll call them and tell them." Damiano hung up the phone and turned to them, "They just found her. I'm calling the police now."

Jason pushed up from the couch and started to pace. His shoulder hurt, and he was sure his neck muscles would be screaming at him later for the jolt he'd received earlier. He was a little more relaxed hearing that they knew where she was until the next call came in less than four minutes later. Upon hearing that news, he sprinted from the room, just in front of Rodrick. They rode the elevator down to the lobby, and Jason ran out of the building quickly, knowing that the other man was tight on his heels. He knew it was up to him to save the woman he loved, and he knew just where she was heading.

Katie stood outside on the corner of the street she'd been

at just yesterday with Jason. Her bank stood before her and she thought of how to get away from the two men. Looking around at the crowded street, she felt the pressure of the knife at her side and wondered how she was going to get out of this.

She'd imagined her whole life that she would have kids someday and grow old with the man she loved. Jason's face crossed her mind and she knew, just like she'd always known, that he was the one she pictured having that family with. He'd always been the one she had pictured spending her life with kids, house, dogs, everything. Realizing she had never gotten the chance to tell him how she really felt, she almost panicked. She had to escape this, just had to, so she could tell him how she felt now and had always felt.

She didn't know what was going to happen to her when these men found out that the daily limit on her card was five thousand and not the enormous amount they were demanding? She knew one thing, she needed to make sure she didn't get back in the van with them. Even if it meant doing something drastic.

She was standing at the ATM, knife to her back, her hands shaking, when all of a sudden, the large man was yanked away from her side. Turning, she watched Jason swinging at the man, as the other man swung his arm towards him, the knife clutched in his hand. She must have screamed because everyone stopped and stared in horror. She watched Jason deflect the blow, using the man's weight to send him reeling off balance against the stone wall. The man recovered quickly and inched his way towards her. She backed up several feet and watched as

Jason stepped between them, blocking the man's path to her.

"Get back, Katie," he yelled over his shoulder.

Just then the other man, Raul, jumped from the van a few feet away and started running towards her, a gun held in his hand. As he ran to her, his eyes kept darting to his partner, watching him fight with Jason.

Katie didn't look at the fight, she couldn't. She needed to do something quickly to help herself, before the man used the gun on her, or worse, Jason. She looked around frantically for a weapon when she noticed a large flower pot sitting next to her foot. She bent down and picked it up and used all her strength to throw it at the man. The clay pot shattered against the side of his skull, sending him flying to the ground in a large, unconscious heap. The gun skidded across the sidewalk and under the van, out of sight.

Now she just needed to get the other two men apart before Jason got hurt. When she got closer to them, she noticed blood all over Jason's face and arms and saw in horror that his hands were covered as well.

She started freaking out! Where had it all come from? Had he been cut? Her breath was coming in quick bursts and she was shaking uncontrollably. She rushed over and stood back, looking for any way to stop them. She needed to get them apart but there wasn't anything else that could help her. Then she heard a shout and looked over to see her father running towards them.

"Hurry, Dad! He has a knife and Jason's hurt!" she yelled in his direction.

Hearing that help was on the way, the other man let down his guard momentarily, and Jason's fist slammed into the side of his head, landing a blow that took the man to his knees. She'd seen him use his Judo in practice several times, and she'd been very impressed. But none of it compared to the street fighting skills she'd just witnessed.

Her father skid to a halt and grabbed the knife from the unconscious man's hands as Katie threw herself into Jason's arms and held on to him, enjoying the feel of him holding her back.

CHAPTER 12

*T*wo hours later, after explaining everything to the police several times, telling them every detail and waiting for it all to be translated back and forth, Jason wished for a shower and some time alone with Katie.

The doctor had come and looked at him, and thankfully he had only had minor cuts from the car glass and none of those needed stitches. His fists were cut and slightly swollen. When he'd looked at himself in the bathroom mirror, he realized he looked like he'd lost a battle with a dozen cats. He'd heard that Dante had it much worse and that he had been rushed to the hospital where he was having surgery to put pins in his left leg and shoulder. Without Dante and Ric, they wouldn't have known where the men had been taking Katie. Jason owed them so much. He was so proud of Katie for maneuvering the men into taking her someplace public and for her quick thinking in showing her brother where they were heading. Without that, well, he didn't want to think about what would have happened.

Not to mention that Rodrick had followed him the dozen blocks to the bank and helped out where he could. For a sixty-year-old man, he had kept up with him pretty well. He'd arrived just in time to see the end of the fight, but Jason knew that he would have gladly jumped in the ring at any time.

Katie's father and brother never left her side the entire time they sat at the police station. Ric had walked to the police station from the hospital. He'd given them the update on Dante and told them that Damiano had rushed to the hospital to be by his son's side. He told Ric to tell them that he would see Katie tomorrow and that he was happy everything was okay.

By the look on Ric's face, Jason knew that Kathleen had been at the hospital, too. He didn't know what Ric thought of the woman anymore, but the sour look on his face told him that he wasn't too pleased to see her there.

He knew that Katie would have wanted to avoid seeing her, so they agreed to visit Dante the next morning, knowing she wouldn't be there.

Jason had almost lost Katie. How could he have been so stupid as to walk them on a public sidewalk, in broad daylight? He never thought that she could be snatched like that. He assumed that they would be safe, but he wouldn't make that mistake again. He knew he didn't want to live without her, he couldn't.

When they walked out of the police station several hours later, they rode in a taxi cab with Rodrick to the hotel where Rodrick and Ric had been staying since their arrival.

Ric had gone and retrieved their rental car and backpacks for them an hour earlier. He'd even gotten them a single room for the night in the same hotel. Jason had known Ric his whole life, and they respected each other. He could tell that Ric had known the second he'd seen them together that Katie and his relationship had changed.

Ric had shaken his hand at the police station. Then he had hugged him and quietly said, "Welcome to the family, bro." Jason just smiled and had put his arm around Katie.

Now they headed up to their room to get some well-needed rest. The second they entered the room alone, he turned and just held onto her. He couldn't remember a hug feeling this good in his entire life. He knew he must smell like blood and probably had enough on him that people could easily mistake him for a vampire who'd just eaten, but he held her until she stopped crying. Then he realized tears had escaped his eyes as well.

"It's okay, you're okay," he whispered to her, but when she didn't stop crying right away, he asked, "What, what's wrong, baby?"

"I thought…" she pulled back and looked at him as he wiped her tears away gently with his fingers. "I thought I would never see you again, that I wouldn't be able to tell you how much I love you."

"You don't have to tell me, I already know. It's the same way I feel about you. Katie, I don't want to live a day without you." He looked into her eyes. "We've been friends forever and I can't imagine a day without you. I don't want to be without you ever again."

She looked at him, then took his hand and started walking him backward.

"Katie?" he pulled her to a stop. "I pretty much just asked you to marry me."

"I know, but we need a shower before I answer you." She smiled and tugged until he followed her into the bathroom where she started removing his soiled clothing quickly.

Giving in, he laughed and started pulling her clothes off more quickly as they kissed.

They walked into the large shower and slowly enjoyed cleaning every inch of each other under the warm spray.

He noticed some bruises on her arms when he ran his soapy hands over her. Then he turned her around and shampooed her hair, slowly rubbing his fingers on her scalp, causing her to moan with delight.

"You know; I can get used to you shampooing my hair. It feels so, mmmm."

"Good," he chuckled. "I love the feel of it. I like the shorter style, it suits you."

Once he was done with her hair, he ran his hands down her shoulders. Pulling her back against him, he brushed his fingers over her chest, sending small goose bumps over her skin. She shivered and rolled her head back with her eyes closed as she leaned back against him.

He continued his downward path over her stomach, lower, until he touched her and she grabbed his arms to steady herself. He watched her eyes close. He turned her and took her lips in a passionate kiss that he never wanted to end.

When the water turned cool, he pulled her out and wrapped a towel around her. He walked her backward while drying her face and hair with the towel. She laughed and tried to pull him down for another kiss.

"No, no, turn around, I have to finish drying you off."
He smiled wickedly, knowing just what she needed.

She looked at him and smiled, then turned so her bare
back was facing him. Slowly he rubbed the dry towel over
her shoulders, taking care to move down each arm. Then
he moved back to the middle of her back, running kisses
down her shoulders. She dropped her head forward, so he
would have better access. Then he ran the towel over her
perfect rear end, and bending down, he placed a light kiss
on each cheek.

She smiled as he used his hands to push her forward,
so she was bent over, holding herself up on the bed. Then
he used his knees and hands to spread her legs wider,
giving himself access to her. He used the towel and lightly
dried every inch of her legs, roaming upwards until he let
the soft cotton rub against her, causing her to moan. He
used his fingers against her wet skin, listening to the slickness that he'd caused as he rubbed her until she was
panting with want.

"Please, Jason,"

Then he stood behind her and grabbing her hips, positioned himself just at her entrance.

"Tell me that you'll marry me, Katie." He held himself
just outside her, so she could feel the light pressure.

"Yes, of course, I'll marry you. Now, Jason,"

He slid into her and quickly lost his self-control,
moving faster until they were both out of breath.

The next morning just past nine o'clock, there was a light
knock on their door. Thinking it was her father or Ric, she

175

opened it without looking through the peep-hole and then tried to slam it shut again, quickly. Her mother was too fast for her, and she moved her foot into the doorway, holding it opened.

"Move your foot!" Katie growled.

"No, I'm not going anywhere until we talk" Her mother crossed her arms and glared at her like it had all been her fault.

Katie thought it would be childish of her to slam the door harder on her foot, so instead, she walked back into the room, deciding to try a different tactic of ignoring her.

Katie still had yet to blow dry her hair from her morning shower, so she walked into the restroom and turned on the blow dryer, sufficiently silencing anything her mother had to say to her.

She watched out of the corner of her eye as her mother walked into the room and closed the door quietly behind her, then she heard her start up a conversation with Jason in the next room.

Her mother had always looked younger than her years, and her rich, shoulder-length chestnut hair had been something Katie always wished she had. She was tan and toned, no doubt due to the many hours playing tennis, one of her favorite pastimes. She was wearing a simple sundress today, something Katie had never seen her in. She'd always worn the latest and most expensive outfits when she'd been married to her father. This dress flowed and looked very relaxing, a term she'd never used before to describe her mother. She could see the simple changes in her mother; she looked healthier, a little thinner, and happier.

The traitor that was the man she loved actually talked

to her mother the entire time she was drying her hair. She was having second thoughts about marrying him when she realized she couldn't postpone turning off the blow dryer any longer. Her hair was dry and on the verge of frizzing if she didn't get it away from the heat.

Katie walked into the room and she could see the tension on Jason's face. Maybe he wasn't completely a traitor after all. She could tell he was still upset at her mother and that did something for her. Walking over to him, she easily walked into his arms and looked at her mother.

"I know you didn't want to see me yesterday. I tried to give you some time…"

"We're getting married," Katie interrupted and watched the surprise on her mother's face. Then her mother smiled, and Katie wondered why she looked like she had always known that they would be together.

"Congratulations," her mother said after a few seconds of silence. She looked truly happy for them and it kind of upset Katie. She was hoping to shock her mother, but instead, she felt like she'd walked into one of her mother's well-thought-out plans.

Katie nodded.

"Oh, I can't wait to help plan your wedding. I've been dreaming about it your whole life. We can have an elaborate wedding back in Boston, so all your friends can attend. You won't have to worry about anything, I'll take care of…"

"No mother, you won't take care of anything. Besides, we don't have any more friends in Boston, thanks to you. Did you honestly think you could waltz in here and start playing mom by planning our wedding? That I would allow you to have anything to do with something so important?" Katie laughed. "Like I would ever take wedding planning advice from a woman who doesn't know the least bit about what a real marriage is." She turned and walked over to the window to look out at the city.

"Really, Katie, this is all so very childish."

"Childish?" Katie turned on her and looked at the woman who had spent years lying to everyone she loved. Lying to Katie her entire life.

Katie was built like her mother. They were both short with toned arms and legs, but where her mother's skin was lighter, Katie's had always had an olive darkness to it. She'd assumed it was from her grandparents or that it had been passed down from some other unknown source. Now she knew all too well that she'd gotten it, along with her dark hair and eyes, from her father's Italian heritage.

"You think I'm being childish?" Katie walked towards her and looked her right in the face.

"Get out! I don't want to ever see you again."

"Don't you take that tone with me. I'm still your mother and I deserve respect."

"No, you lost all my respect, and you haven't done anything yet to show me you deserve any of it back."

Her mother glanced over at Jason and Katie understood her meaning.

"Him?" Katie looked at Jason, who looked like he wanted to be anywhere but there. "I already know that you hired him to find me. You didn't do anything but give him money, so he could accomplish the task."

"Why do you think I hired him? He's not a professional. No offense, Jason."

"None taken." He smiled at them both and tried to

edge his way out of the room, only to come up short when Katie grabbed his arm and held him still.

"I hired him because I knew what you needed. What you've always needed." Her mother started pacing the small room. Throwing her hands up, she turned back to Katie. "Do you think I raised you all these years and didn't know what was best for you?"

"I don't understand."

"Katie," she walked over and grabbed her shoulders, "I love you, you're my daughter, and no matter what the circumstances are, that will never change. I *loved* Rodrick and as much as it hurts you to hear it, I'm in love with Damiano. I've been in love with Damiano from the moment I met him. I know that what I did was wrong and I'm very sorry I hurt so many people. But I'm happy now, and I just want you to be happy, too."

Katie walked over and sat on the edge of the bed. She didn't feel like hearing anymore, but her mother sat next to her and took her face into her hands.

"Katie, I love you, I'm so very proud of the strength you've shown in the last few weeks. I wish I had some of that strength years ago to do what I had needed to. Instead, I lived a lie and hurt the people I loved. You know how it is when you fall in love with someone. How it totally consumes you and you'd do anything to be with them. No matter the cost."

Katie watched as a tear rolled down her mother's face.

"I'm not proud of myself for deceiving everyone. Damiano has forgiven me and I can't tell you how happy I am that he still wants to be with me. I just hope that someday you can understand why I did what I did and maybe then you can forgive me."

"I can't forgive you. I don't know if I will ever be able to forgive you." Katie saw the hurt flash in her mother's eyes.

"I understand; you have that right." She pulled back a little. "I hope that you won't shut me out of your life and pray that you won't take it out on your brothers or your fathers."

Katie laughed, "I would never treat them bad. They've been hurt just like me." She turned and looked her mother in the eyes. "I've had a lot of time to think about things this last year and I realized that they're in the same boat as I am. How could I ever be mad at them?"

Kathleen smiled a little. "I'm very proud of you. Will you give me a chance to make things right with you?"

Katie looked at her mother, really looked at her and saw something she'd never seen her entire life. She noticed for the first time that her mother was just a woman. Katie had always built her up, tried to make her something she could never be, perfect.

"I'm not saying I can ever understand why you did what you've done." She looked over at Jason, then back at her mother. "But I will *try* to give you a second chance." She tried not to grit her teeth when she'd said that.

Kathleen jumped up and pulled Katie into a hug.

"I'm not saying everything is going to be like it used to be." Katie tried to pull away. She was trying to be okay with being in the same room as the woman she felt she could no longer trust.

"Oh, I know, I understand. I just want you to do what makes you happy." But she could see her mother's face light up and when she looked around the room for Jason, she noticed him leaning against the wall, smiling at her.

"Now," her mother brushed off a few tears that had rolled down her cheeks, then she straightened her dark slacks with her hands, "shall we go meet your fathers and brothers?"

Katie laughed.

Less than an hour later, they walked into Dante's hospital room. Her father, Rodrick, her half-brother Ric, her biological father Damiano, and her biological brother Dante were all there.

She had met Damiano outside in the waiting area before. When she had stepped into the room and seen him for the first time, she realized where she'd received the dark curly hair, deep, dark eyes, and the olive skin coloring from. Damiano was a sturdy looking man. He was tall and looked like he spent more time in a gym than in the suit he was wearing. She could instantly see all the answers to the questions she'd had over the years. Her nose, her chin, and even her ears came from the man standing before her.

Damiano instantly hugged her in a warm embrace, and she felt a little overwhelmed.

"I'm so happy that you are okay." He whispered it and she thought his voice had cracked a little. "You look so much like your Nonna. Full of spitfire and spunk." He patted her cheek with his hand and turned to take hold of his wife's hand.

She didn't know what to say. She supposed she was in shock, so she just nodded her head and smiled. Grabbing a hold of Jason's hand in a death grip, she tried to pull him closer to her.

Walking into Dante's hospital room a few minutes later, she saw Dante sitting up in the hospital bed, and upon seeing her full brother for the first time, her steps faltered.

There was no mistaking the fact that they were made from the same mold. Dante was built a lot like Ric, but Katie and Dante's features, along with their coloring, were identical.

She was amazed at the love that radiated from the room.

Katie watched Damiano and her mother. When she saw the looks the couple gave each other, she instantly knew that there was more love between them then there had ever been between her father and her mother. You'd have to be blind not to see it.

When she turned and looked at Dante, he smiled with kindness and she could tell he was happy she was there. She could also tell he was on some serious pain pills since his eyes were dull and droopy.

He'd given so much to try to save her, and she realized he must be in terrible pain.

"Don't worry, I'm on all kinds of medications, I can hardly feel anything." He smiled at her with a goofy lopsided smile.

"Am I that transparent?" she asked, sitting next to him.

"No, we just have such similar faces, it's like reading my own emotions." They both laughed.

Ric and Rodrick had been hanging in the background, watching, until Katie turned and walked to both of them. She hugged her father and whispered, "I love you, Daddy," and she felt him melt in her arms.

"You scared us." Ric walked up and hugged her. She had said what she had wanted to say to him yesterday. For as long as she would live, he would always be her big brother.

She had been overly excited to hear the news yesterday that Roberta was seven weeks pregnant. She was going to be an aunt next spring. She couldn't get over the idea of her big brother being a dad.

Jason walked up beside her then and took her hand in his. "Do you want to tell them or should I?" He smiled.

"Oh, yeah," she smiled up at him and looked into the room full of her family. "Jason and I are getting married." Everyone smiled and started to walk forward to congratulate them when she interrupted with "tomorrow."

She had the satisfaction of seeing her mother's smile falter before she was engulfed in a hug from her family.

EPILOGUE

K atie stood on the beach in a simple cream-colored summer dress. Her bare feet felt good in the hot sand as she walked towards the people she cared about the most.

Jason stood by the priest in his rolled-up dress pants and white dress shirt, which was unbuttoned a little at the top. Katie kept his eyes and smile in focus as she walked the few feet on the arm of her Dad, who looked very dashing and couldn't stop smiling at her.

Her brother Ric stood next to Jason with a huge smile on his face, as well. She wished that Roberta could be there next to him but knew that the short notice wasn't sufficient. They had plans to visit them in Portland this Christmas.

Although she would have liked nothing better than to exclude her mother, she stood a few feet away next to Damiano, silently crying into a white tissue. She was surprised to learn that she had an aunt; Florentina Damiano's younger sister. The stout woman stood next to her brother, and in Katie's opinion, looked like she was in shock. She had yet to talk to the woman but was happy that she could make it today.

She knew Dante was still in the hospital recovering and they had plans to visit him later that night before they headed back down the coast for their honeymoon.

When they reached where everyone stood, Rodrick stopped and kissed her and whispered, "You will always be my daughter. I love you, sweetie."

Katie almost lost it then, but she took a deep breath and kissed him on the cheek as he handed her off to Jason.

Then she looked into the bluest eyes she'd ever seen and was happy knowing that she would be looking at them for the rest of her life.

Her careful planning had been ruined, overthrown by the two people she was watching get married. The man was tall and strong, and the girl reminded her too much of her grandmother, which only confirmed her decision to halt her plan of attack. No, she couldn't in clear conscience continue to scheme against someone who looked so much like Nonna.

She would have to do some thinking on the next steps she needed to take. Her goal was the same, but her methods needed to be changed.

She'd been using Kathleen to get information on her daughter's whereabouts. After all, the woman wasn't really a good mother. Not like she'd been to Dante.

Thinking about Dante, she knew he deserved to be head of the family and she silently wished she could be next to him in the hospital as he recovered. She longed for that day when he would know everything she'd done for him, everything she'd sacrificed. Because of the love she had for him, much like a mother to her only child, her only desire was to see him succeed. Katie Derby was just a bump in the path to his greatness. She would make sure he took the power that was due him, the wealth, and the family rights.

There were, after all, other methods for accomplishing her desires, but she had a few minor details to dispose of first. She watched the young couple walk towards her and when her brother said her name, she finally stepped forward to meet her niece for the first time.

If you've enjoyed this book, please consider leaving a review where you purchased it. Thanks! --Jill

*A*irlea walked out of the hospital just after midnight. Her shift had ended an hour earlier, but she'd been so caught up helping her latest patient, Anna, she'd been late leaving work. Anna had been in a fire just over a month ago, and seventy percent of her little, eight-year-old body had been badly burned. Her little arms and legs had the telltale signs of scarring, and even though she was still wrapped up tight in bandages, Airlea knew what was underneath them.

Getting the little girl to trust her had been easy, keeping her happy wasn't. Airlea knew the road ahead for Anna was going to be a difficult one and she knew by the time she got done, Anna wasn't going to like her. Tonight, Anna had gotten her first glimpse at what was ahead of her. Airlea had pushed the little girl until there were big fat tears rolling down her perfect little cheeks.

Being a physical therapist was what Airlea was born to do. She loved helping others heal and recover after something major had knocked them down. She looked at it as a rebirth experience for her patients. Most of them came out the other side a changed person. Almost all came out a better person than they'd been when they'd experienced their setbacks.

She was walking the same roads she'd walked for the last five years of her life. Her tiny apartment was only two blocks from the hospital in Igoumenitsa, Greece. She'd been born and raised just outside of Venice, Italy, but shortly after finishing school, she'd moved to Greece when she'd been offered a full-time position at the hospital here. She'd enjoyed her time ever since arriving.

She had friends and had even had a few relationships, her latest ending a little over a month ago. Angelo Ernesto had been everything Airlea had ever wanted in a man. He'd been caring, patient, kind, very good looking, and a doctor. That was until she'd allowed him to move in with her after they had been dating for six months. Then everything had changed.

It had taken less than a week for her to see the side of himself that he'd been hiding. The jealousy and temper brought on by the smallest things had been the reason she'd asked him to move out less than a month after he'd moved in. Now when she walked by him in the halls of the hospital, she tried to avoid talking to him.

How could something so beautiful be so rotten on the inside? She'd learned a valuable lesson with him. Angelo still called her sometimes, but she'd gotten to the point where she didn't answer his calls anymore. Every call she did answer would start out with him apologizing, then it would escalate to him raising his voice about why she wouldn't take him back. She just didn't want to deal with him anymore.

She'd made it halfway up the stairs outside her apartment before she saw Angelo sitting on the steps. She rolled her eyes; she wasn't in the mood to deal with him anymore.

"Hi," he said, standing up and matching her steps to follow her the rest of the way to her apartment door.

"Listen, Angelo, I'm really tired. I've just gotten off my shift and I'm heading straight to bed. Can we talk tomorrow, instead?" She hunted in her bag for her keys, not even glancing in his direction.

When she reached her door, he pushed her until her back was up against the hardwood, the doorknob thrust painfully against her hip. His hands held her shoulders back.

"Damn it, Airlea, if you never talk to me, how can we make this all better?" He growled.

"Let go of me!" When he didn't, she dropped her bag and tried to push him back a step. He didn't budge. "We are not going to work this out. Don't you get it? I don't want to work it out. It just didn't work, move on."

"I can't believe you're being such a bitch about this. You kick me out with some lame-ass excuse and now you won't even talk to me." He held her, looking down into her eyes. "If you'd just give me a chance." He started moving his head towards her, leaning in as if he was coming in for a kiss.

She turned her head away. "Get off me, Angelo. I've told you, it's over. Get off!" She pushed him again, this time catching him off guard a little. He took two steps back and glared at her as she slid her keys in the door and quickly stepped inside, leaving her bag outside her door.

"You think this is over?" he screamed to her closed

door. "I have pull at the hospital. Don't think I won't use it." She watched him through her peep-hole as he picked up her bag and walked away. She relaxed against her locked door, very glad that the scene was over. So, she'd lost her scrubs and her extra pair of shoes. She knew she could get them back if she just talked to him, but she didn't want to and the items didn't really matter.

The next day at work, she was called into the director's office. As she stood in front of his large metal desk, she kicked herself for the fool she was.

"Miss Rossi is this your bag?" Mr. Lutz wasn't one of those 'hands-on' kind of directors. He was strict and very old-school. Any explanation she might have given as to how he'd gotten her bag and who had taken it and why would fall on deaf ears.

"Yes, sir." She braced herself for whatever was going to come next.

"Can you explain this?" He opened the bag and she watched as a dozen pill bottles fell out. She recognized some of the names on the labels and her mouth fell open. The bottles of medicine had been missing for over a week. Employees of the hospital had received memos all week long about the missing medication.

An hour later she walked out of the hospital, the contents of her locker in a box tucked under her arm, and her dignity lost forever. She assured herself the entire short walk home that she would never trust a man again.

CHAPTER 1

*D*ante threw the glass across the room and smiled a little when he heard it shatter on the wood door. His mother stood next to his bed and crossed her arms, glaring down at him. He knew he was acting childish, and he didn't care. The pain had fogged his mind to the point that nothing else mattered.

It had been two days since he'd been released from the hospital, and so far he'd only had about three hours of sleep. He knew his mother and aunt had the best intentions for him, but he couldn't stand them being around all the time, seeing him like this. So he'd acted out the only way he knew how, by throwing things and yelling at them.

He looked up from the bed he'd spent the last two days in and noticed his mother's left eye twitching, something that only happened when she was truly pissed at him.

"Dante Damiano Cardone, I'm so ashamed of you right now. You will not behave like this when Miss Rossi gets here, do you understand me?" Her voice was low and he could almost feel the vibration from it. He was saved from answering his mother when his aunt rushed into the room.

"What's going on in here?" She moved over to his side and grabbed his hand gently. Her dark gray hair was long and flowed close around her face. She was a stout woman who held herself like she had a lot of power.

"Dante are you in much pain?" Her English wasn't very good, but she spoke it none the less since his mother had set the rule many years ago that when she was in the house, they spoke English. Something even his aunt had obeyed for the last twenty-seven years. It hadn't been hard for them to follow the rule in the past since his mother had only been in the house a few weeks out of every year. But now, she was living there full-time and he could tell his aunt was having a hard time following the rule and tolerating the other woman in her house.

Florentina Cardone was in her late fifties and the younger sister of Dante's father, Damiano, though she acted like she was the older one. She always seemed to be in charge of him, at least when his mother wasn't around.

The house Dante had grown up in was very large and had been handed down for over five generations. His father had spent his first million refurbishing his parents' small home and turning it into what it was today—a mansion. The acres of olive tree groves and vineyards spread out around the large tan, red-roofed place which sat like a beacon in the green fields of rolling hills. The view was spectacular, something he had missed while he had lived in the States over the last few years. But, since his return home, he had yet to enjoy any of it.

He tried to sit up a little and was reminded of the sharp pain shooting down his left side. The pins in his leg that started just above his knee towards the outside of his thigh, and the pain in his shoulder caused such immense pain, his vision actually blurred.

He didn't blame his sister, Katie, for his injuries. After all, it had been her kidnappers that had rammed their vehicle into his own. He was just grateful that his half-brother, Ric; Ric's father, Rodrick; and Katie's new husband, Jason, had been there to help save his newly found sister from the two men, hell-bent on kidnapping her.

Dante had found out the truth about his hidden half-brother, Ric, when he was in college in the States. He'd been raised to think his mother had an affair while in college and had Ric then, but just last year the truth had finally come out that his mother had been married to Ric's father and actually had two children. Ric was almost six years older than Dante. Katie, who had been raised by Rodrick Derby as his own, was, in fact, his full-blooded sister. Katie was almost three years younger than him.

He'd finally gotten to meet Katie for the first tie, at the hospital the day after his accident. He couldn't really remember meeting her that day, but she'd come back the next few days before she and her new husband had left on their honeymoon. He'd gotten to know her and Jason, quite well by the time he'd finally been released from the hospital almost two weeks later.

His mother had not only cheated his father out of a daughter, but she'd deceived them all. The entire time he had been growing up, he'd been told that her absence from the family was because her parents in the States didn't condone his parent's relationship. When the truth was, she had a completely separate family that she was spending her time with.

Growing up, he'd seen her as often as one would a distant relative. His aunt had filled the role of mother for most of his life, and he could tell that now that his mother was in the house full-time, his aunt despised the fact that her brother hadn't kicked her to the curb after the truth had come out. But Damiano had been adamant about his views and feelings towards Kathleen. Shortly after Kathleen had dissolved her marriage to Rodrick, Dante's parents had officially been married.

"Dante, you need to not work yourself up so much. Here, you need to take your medicine. You drink the soup I made for you, then take these." His aunt held up the bottle of medicine he'd been ready to throw at the door after the glass.

He might be able to deny his mother, but he couldn't say no to his aunt. Looking into those dark chocolate eyes, he was reminded of his upbringing and knew he needed to obey the short woman who had raised him like her own.

"Florentina, maybe you can talk some sense into my son." His mother uncrossed her arms and walked to the doorway. "I expect him to behave when Miss Rossi gets here."

"Who is this Miss Rossi?" His aunt asked.

"Remember? She is the nurse I've hired to take care of Dante. She's a specialist in physical therapy. She's the one that's going to get him on his feet again." His mother started to walk out the door and he swore he heard her say. "Even if it kills him."

Airlea Rossi was running late. Her little car sputtered and coughed up the long, muddy driveway. Her GPS told her the house was two miles ahead, but the roadway was so rugged, she didn't think her little Saab would make the trek.

Finally admitting defeat, she pulled over into the grass. Getting out of her car, she looked around and all she could see were trees and deep green, rolling fields.

Picking up her phone from her seat, she checked the GPS one more time. The little red arrow pointed in front of her, and less than two miles down the road was the blue dot that marked her destination. Tossing the phone back into her car, she stomped her foot.

"Skata!" she screamed into the field.

Just then she heard a noise and looking over her shoulder. An old, beat-up pickup truck was bumping up the lane behind her.

Waving her arms, she felt relief when the older gentleman stopped beside her car. He wore dirty overalls and had a big hat on his head.

"Hello? Are you lost?" He asked in Italian.

"Yes, I'm looking for the Cardone residence," she answered easily.

She watched as the man took off his big hat and ran his forearm across his sweaty forehead. He had a full head of very dark curly hair and was younger than she had first thought.

"What do you want at the Cardones?" He asked.

"I am the nurse hired to help with their son." She smiled.

"Well, why didn't you say this, to begin with?" He put back on his hat and got out of the truck. "Your car won't make it up the drive. I'll drive you the rest of the way." He walked around the truck. "Do you have bags?"

"Yes." She felt uneasy about leaving her car in a field alongside a dirt road. Even though the car was a few years old, it didn't deserve to be deserted like this. "What shall I do?" she asked as she motioned to her car.

"Well, I can have someone come and tow it up to the main house if you want. Then we can make sure when you leave, that we get you back down the hill safely. Usually, the road isn't this bad, but we've had rain the last four days. The mud makes the road become too much for anything but the truck here to get through." He patted the truck.

Then he helped her get her two bags out of the back of her car and tossed them in the back of the truck. She rolled up her windows and locked her car, making sure to grab her purse and cell phone.

"I'm Airlea," she said holding out her hand.

"I'm Damiano Cardone." He took her smaller hand in his and shook it politely.

"Oh!" She gasped, realizing that this was her new employer. She felt her face flush with embarrassment. She'd assumed he'd been a hired hand, or just a passing farmer, not the owner of a million-dollar, world-renowned corporation.

They got into the truck and started heading up the muddy lane. She sat there and thought about how her mother had fibbed to get her this job. She couldn't blame her mother; after all, it had sounded like the deal of the century.

"Airlea, you need to get out of town for a while and regroup. This job in Italy is perfect for you. The wealth in

the Cardone family goes back for many years, and they are very well known. Their son was in a very bad accident a few weeks ago and they are looking for a nurse with your qualifications to help the boy mend, to get him back on his feet, something you were made to do. Plus, it pays more for a few months' worth of work than you made all last year working at the hospital."

She'd sat across from her mother, in her small apartment and chewed her bottom lip, thinking that she did need to get out of town for a while. Things had not turned out well with Angelo and since she'd lost her job, she didn't know what was left for her in Greece.

"Mama, what do I need to know about this job? How old is the boy? What are his injuries?" She'd tried to pry information out of her mother.

"Oh, I don't know these details," her mother had waived her off, "you can find out when you get there. The only thing you need to know besides being a great nurse is how to speak English. You took two years of it in school, you will be fine."

"I almost failed two years, you mean! Did you tell them I spoke good English?" She felt like screaming.

"Yes, Airlea, you will be fine." Her mother continued to look at the newspaper in front of her.

So, less than two days later, she had packed up all of her belongings and left them in storage to come to Italy.

"I guess I'll be helping your son recover from his accident." She looked across the seat at Damiano.

"Yes, Dante is having a hard time recovering. I don't know how much my wife told you over the phone, but he isn't adjusting well. I think he doesn't like his medicine." He smiled over at her.

"Well, it can be tricky getting the right dosage and the right prescription. Is he in a lot of pain?" She wished he would give more detail of the accident but didn't want to pry.

"I suppose so. I keep myself busy most days since it's almost harvest time for my olive grove, but my wife, Kathleen, tells me he is being unbearable." He chuckled.

The rest of the drive was a quiet one. She didn't know what to say to the man. She desperately wished for more information. She held onto the door handle as the truck bumped up the muddy lane.

Finally, they turned a corner and she saw the house for the first time.

It was a huge half-stone, a half-stucco house that sat at the top of a large hill. The grass and trees around it were well maintained, and she could just make out a large swimming pool with a pool house to the side as they pulled up.

The stone archway held a balcony that ran across the front of the house and down both sides, with ornate black iron railings. There were huge stone pillars that held up the balcony and stopped waist high on the second level. Each pillar was topped with a clay pot filled with bright red flowers. Deep, wide steps led up to the tall retreat. There were a half dozen French doors along the front and the same number along the sides, both upstairs and down.

The truck stopped in front of a large garage with six bays. Several doors were open, and she could see other well-maintained expensive cars parked inside.

"I'll just go and see about getting your car up here. You can go on in and make yourself at home. Kathleen will be somewhere around. I'll bring your bags inside." He pointed to a door, just under another balcony.

She watched him walk into the garage, she turned and looking around the yard. The last hundred feet of the drive had been done in deep red bricks and the walkway to the house had large stone steps that sat down in the well-groomed grass. Taking the pathway, she had just reached the doorway when she heard a large crash come from the open doors above her. When she heard a low rumble of cuss words, her heart skipped, knowing that someone had just fallen. Her nurse's instincts kicked in and she dropped her purse and rushed up the large, wide stairs.

She ran through the opened doors before she had time to think of what she was doing.

There, in the middle of the floor, lay the most handsome man she'd ever seen. He looked very large, sprawled out lying on his front side, and then she noticed that he was completely naked.

ALSO BY JILL SANDERS

The Pride Series

Finding Pride

Discovering Pride

Returning Pride

Lasting Pride

Serving Pride

Red Hot Christmas

My Sweet Valentine

Return To Me

Rescue Me

The Secret Series

Secret Seduction

Secret Pleasure

Secret Guardian

Secret Passions

Secret Identity

Secret Sauce

The West Series

Loving Lauren

Taming Alex

Holding Haley

Missy's Moment

Breaking Travis

Roping Ryan

Wild Bride

Corey's Catch

Tessa's Turn

The Grayton Series

Last Resort

Someday Beach

Rip Current

In Too Deep

Swept Away

High Tide

Lucky Series

Unlucky In Love

Sweet Resolve

Best of Luck

A Little Luck

Silver Cove Series

Silver Lining

French Kiss

Happy Accident

Hidden Charm

A Silver Cove Christmas

Entangled Series – Paranormal Romance

The Awakening

The Beckoning

The Ascension

St. Helena Vineyard Kindle Worlds

Where I Belong

Haven, Montana Series

Closer to You

Never Let Go

Pride Oregon Series

A Dash of Love

My Kind of Love

For a complete list of books: http://JillSanders.com

ABOUT THE AUTHOR

Jill Sanders is *The New York Times* and *USA Today* bestselling author of Sweet Small-Town Contemporary Romance Series, Thrilling Romantic Suspense Series, Sexy Western Romance Series, and Intriguing Paranormal Romance novels. She continues to lure new readers with her sweet and sexy stories. Her books are available in every English-speaking country and in audiobooks as well as being translated into different languages.

Born as an identical twin to a large family, she was raised in the Pacific Northwest and later relocated to Colorado for college and a successful IT career before discovering her talent as a writer. She now makes her home along the Emerald Coast in Florida where she enjoys the beach, hiking, swimming, wine-tasting, and of course writing.

26939255R00118

Made in the USA
Lexington, KY
03 January 2019